To Build a Better World

By Jack MacLeod

TOH Press

To Build a Better World

by Jack MacLeod

Copyright 2016 © Jack MacLeod and Cynthia Smith

All Rights Reserved

Published in Canada by TOH Press
ISBN 978-0-9921227-6-8

About the Author

Jack MacLeod (aka McLeod) was born in Regina, Saskatchewan in 1932. He earned a BA and MA in economics at the University of Saskatchewan before taking a Ph.D. in political science at the University of Toronto where he taught from 1959-1996. An experience in Budapest during the Hungarian Revolution in 1956 led him to begin writing political journalism, some of which appeared in the Globe and Mail, the Toronto Star, Saturday Night, Books in Canada, Canadian Forum and the Journal of Canadian Studies as well as on the CBC. MacLeod published several academic works with University of Toronto Press, Oxford University Press and McClelland and Stewart and two political science textbooks. His two previous novels, *Zinger and Me* and *Going Grand* were on the bestseller lists. His third Zinger novel, *Uproar*, has recently been republished in response to popular demand. Both *Zinger and Me* and *Uproar* won honorable mention for the Leacock Medal.

He is married to Cynthia Smith and together they divide their time between homes in Toronto and Muskoka. They rejoice in three children and six grandchildren.

For my wife, Cynthia.

"Courage, my friends...
'Tis not too late to build a better world."

Tommy Douglas

I

When Jamie McRae travelled home to Saskatchewan for his father's funeral he did not feel sad, only a rather calm detachment, fulfilling a duty more irksome than satisfying. Funerals are supposed to console the living as much as celebrate the dead, but he didn't feel any great need for consolation, only the itch of a desire to understand. It was hard for him to see any significance or purpose to the forlorn existence of this man, this stranger he'd known all his life. How odd to discover that he didn't so much dislike his father as merely pity him.

The father always remained something of a mystery to the son. One of the questions Jamie had lived with all his life was what could be wrong with him that his father so often seemed to ignore or disparage him? If his father saw so little in the boy to approve of, how could he regard himself as a good or worthwhile person? It was painful to admit that they'd never much liked each other. Jamie had always wanted his father to love him, but wondered if he ever did. Was this deep emotional trough his own fault, or something lacking in the father? Or both?

It's curious how death often signals a beginning rather than an end. Probably it is the same for all sons, the passing of a parent giving the child a new lease on life and an urge to re-assess both the images of the past and the prospects of an altered future. Awaiting the funeral ceremony he felt regret and some twinges of guilt but little remorse, more a feeling of liberation from the frowning burdens of past failures.

Although he sat in the the first pew staring straight ahead, his facial features stern and composed, threads of conflicting thoughts unnerved him. Was he really alike and close to this cold slab of a father? Did he ever really conenct with this man or share views, traits, feelings, love? He felt uncertain and confused. Probably he could find some serious shortcoming in himself that diminished his emotions. The signature phrase of the fine writer Mavis Gallant re-occurred to him: awareness of "loss and bewilderment." He felt adrift and weirdly disembodied, as though his real self was floating on the ceiling and observing his other vacant self with disdain. He was conscious, in short, of his own emptiness.

Combing through his memories as carefully as he could, he never found the missing piece of the puzzle that was his parent. Lorne Cameron McRae had not seemed an entirely cold man, for he was well liked, even popular with many people, particularly his male friends and drinking buddies. Jamie's older brother Roy had apparently got on with their father well enough, incurring much less of the old man's displeasure than the younger boy. But where was Roy now when he was needed to help sort things out? Together they might have compared their shared recollections into a more coherent pattern and helped each other to assemble a more clear picture of what had been their family.

But even taken together, memories can be fallible and uncertain guides, with events coloured or eroded by time and wishfulness and shifting emotions. What seemed fleeting and inconsequential to one might be freighted with meaning for the other. Each member of a family inevitably will clutch at different and contradictory recollections. Memory is a ghost that whispers half-truths. It seemed to Jamie, as he prepared for the funeral service, that like statistics, there are lies, damned lies, and families. No one's life is a single hard truth that can easily provide understanding of that illusive organism, a bloodline of people living and dying together as a discordant ensemble.

When he'd walked back into his parents' house on Montague Street in Regina, his father's absence lifted a heavy and depressing weight from the rooms. Everything seemed smaller, of course, the house, the street, the old and familiar furniture, but that is the usual reaction in returning to former surroundings once so ample and now so diminished. It was not merely a shrinkage of space that pressed in on him but the apparent smallness of the lives lived here, cramped and narrow lives of ordinary disappointment. He was startled to find that these truncated lives had once seemed to him normal, but now they were ended he could see them more clearly and banish them from his conscience if not from his mind. In some measure he felt absolved, perhaps set free. This strengthened him to face the funeral.

To conduct the service, Jamie had engaged a dour Presbyterian clergyman who, it turned out, had never met his father but had questioned several of McRae's friends for information and perspective on what to say about him in the eulogy. None was much help, nor was Jamie, so the Reverend MacGregor pieced together a formal stream of well intentioned platitudes embellished with phrases like, "not regular in his attendance at church but a good Christian", "a loving husband and good family man", "a great go-getter salesman", and "a former athlete, a man's man". None of these descriptions seemed to the son much more than the usual tags which might be tied to the toe of any luckless corpse, but he was grateful that the preacher could string them out into a plausible ten minutes of sonorous puffery which satisfied the occasion and offended nobody. He squirmed through some gloomy hymns and, when invited to speak, declined with a downcast shake of his head. Some in the small congregation thought he was too overcome with grief to trust his voice, which suited him just fine. The Reverend announced the address of the McRae house where guests would be received and the organ, only slightly out of tune, played a brisk recessional as though everyone would be relieved to see the proceedings conclude.

The house meant little or nothing to Jamie. He had not grown up here, it being merely the most recent place his parents had lived following a series of frequent moves from various apartments and rented bungalows until they fetched up in this shabby-genteel dwelling which Jamie had visited only a few times before now. The confusions of jangled memories floated over him like a grey cloud after the funeral, making it difficult for him to cope with the thirty people who appeared at the house to express sympathy and tuck into beer and coffee, with sandwiches provided by kind neighbours. Mostly they were strangers to him, some with identifiable faces to which he could not quite attach names—or was he the real stranger here himself? These indistinguishable thirty chattered away about what a good man his father was, how proud he had been of his successful son. Proud? He'd never uttered that word to the boy. Successful? An odd word to apply to an estranged son with a stalled career as a junior lecturer at an eastern university, who had only recently dragged his Ph.D. thesis slowly toward a faltering conclusion.

Disoriented and dispirited he made the gesture of trying to be cordial to the bulky clergyman who kept lurking at his elbow. That ponderous worthy was only waiting to be offered an envelope of money for his uplifting services, but also very ready with hopeful Christian advice. To Jamie's idle question of "What shall I do now, Reverend?", he replied that since "this world here below is only life's shadow, a waystage on the road to Eternal Life, one should always contemplate one's sins and vow to do better and just carry on." "You mean, carry on as if nothing has happened?" "Precisely. Nothing of great consequence can happen in this life until you reach its glorious end, re-united with your Maker. So you must carry on, there's the secret, just carry on." Not exactly the sort of counsel to make the spirit soar. Jamie passed the envelope and smiled at the thought that he was actually paying money to this lugubrious twit to spout implacable asininities.

He was saved from the temptation to insult the foolish man by the arrival at his side of the one person in the room he knew and cared about, his favourite uncle, Milt, who silently gave him a bear hug. Milt touched a glass to his and led him to the front door where he paused and said he'd return about seven and take Jamie to dinner at the W. K. Chinese restaurant, an old haunt of theirs.

He was relieved when soon there was a general movement to the door, and when the last guests had departed he sank gratefully into his father's old and worn brown leather armchair and was left alone with his thoughts.

II

Lorne C. McRae was a salesman. He had always been in sales, but was not very good at it. A big man, broad-shouldered and deep-chested with heavy legs, he had been an athlete in school, particularly good at baseball and hockey until he dropped out of the University of Alberta after his sophomore year. Adept with numbers, he had intended to be an engineer but lost interest in schooling after a knee injury knocked him out of sports and bad marks in chemistry brought his grade point average down so that he lost his small scholarship.

Before he quit the University he had met his future wife, Jean Milton, who was studying to be a teacher. She was a slender beauty with very light blonde hair and alert pale blue eyes who had, as they used to say, "class". Her face was fine-featured and pretty with a sweet expression and a rosebud mouth. She wore her thin hair pulled back in a French roll or more often upswept and piled on top of her head encircled by a silk band or narrow bow. Pastel shades were what she usually dressed in, fuzzy sweaters or nubby suits in soft shades of rose or pink or mauve, giving her a subdued, even demure look.

Her mother, now deceased, had been a stern old-fashioned virago more interested in social and charitable events than in her own children, so that it regularly fell to Jean to look after her younger siblings, Eileen and Bill. William Milton, her father, owned an insurance agency and was prosperous, able to put Jean and a brother and sister through university. The father was a gentle and genial man with prematurely grey hair—Jean's hair was almost pure white by the time she was thirty—who tried to warn his eldest daughter that Lorne McRae might not be an ideal choice as a husband, but she was strong willed and determined. Before his knee injury McRae was captain of the hockey team and the tough stocky catcher of the varsity baseball nine. People liked Lorne. He had a smile for everybody even though he was a quiet fellow, what some of the girls called 'the strong silent type'.

Before he dropped out of athletics and out of school his friends believed, and often told Jean, that he would be a whiz of an engineer, probably an electrical engineer, and do very well for himself. The end of his university days, however, made him disappointed and more than a little embittered. Jean was sure that a good wife and a career in sales would lighten his moods and make him a more affable husband. She was a loyal young woman, an optimist, and despite the strictures of her skeptical father, married Lorne when he was twenty-two and she a very inexperienced twenty. They had two sons, Roy, and five years later, Jamie. She doted on both.

As a salesman Lorne always had to scuffle. It never seemed to come easy or naturally to him as he became more guarded and taciturn over the years. A snappy line of patter or peppy sales talk was not for him. Usually he greeted customers in his rumpled second-best brown suit and scuffed shoes, green tie slightly askew. Less well groomed than the other salesmen who tried hard to look smart, his large square face was topped by unparted dark hair combed straight back in a pompadour, his cheap haircut leaving an indented ridge above his ears like a farmer.

Some of his colleagues on the sales staff joked that he should be called "Silent Lorne" or, ironically, "Lippy". His sales pitch, if it could be called that, usually consisted of showing the client a machine and then asking, "Well, how do you like it?" The customer would say, "It's okay, I guess. What will it handle?" And Lorne would smile silently for a moment, then pull out a brochure, hand it over, and mumble something like, "It's all here. Specifications and performance numbers." "Oh," the customer would say. Long silence. "Will it really do all that? Will it live up to these specs?" "Yup." Another long silence, then the customer, probably uneasy that nothing was being said, would start to fill in the blank space by starting to talk about the promised performance in increasingly positive terms and keep talking (while Lorne only smiled and nodded) until he talked himself into it. "Done," he'd say. "Sold." And then scratch his head as he took out his chequebook and wonder how he'd been so easily persuaded, but relieved that he hadn't been fast-talked or high-pressured. A more solid and honest salesman who inspired more confidence he couldn't imagine.

And the other sales staff lingering nearby would shake their heads and laugh that Lippy had done it again.

Unhappily the machinery being sold was from Oliver Farm Equipment Inc., tractors and binders and threshers for which demand fell sharply. Farm incomes dropped as the 1930s wore on. The Depression years were made worse for farmers by prolonged drought and wheat rust and grasshopper plagues as well as plummeting world prices for grain. With the land drying up and blowing away in dust storms, farmers stopped buying machinery and equipment. Oliver sales tanked, and so did Lorne's income which some months dwindled to almost nothing. Saskatchewan, which in the 1930 census had the third highest population of the Canadian provinces, shriveled as people abandoned their farms and moved away, bereft of all hope. Even a quiet salesman could not sell machinery when there were no customers.

By 1932 the McRae family, like the great majority of people in the province, fell on hard times. Probably this quickened in Lorne the urge he'd always felt, a need to find a scheme that would make him rich or at least affluent. As the rest of the salesmen at Oliver quit or were fired, he became the manager of the provincial office and so had a regular salary, but it was pitifully small. After his funeral his son found a big steamer trunk filled with old letters and accounts and papers which on investigation proved to be mostly certificates for penny stocks in long-defunct fly-by-night companies. Worthless. A pile of broken dreams and dashed hopes of riches, dusty trash.

Some of young Jamie's earliest memories were of waking at night to the sound of his parents shouting at each other, fighting about money. At age four or even later at age six he couldn't make much sense of it. The loud fighting alarmed him and also confused him because he had almost no idea of what money meant. To him money was a few pennies to buy candy or five cents to buy an occasional ice cream cone or chocolate bar, but clearly it was an important thing to his parents and a cause of conflict. His mother seemed to find it distressing. Jean's brother and sister, she often said, were successful and had money. She was embarrassed that she could not go home to visit her family, even if she could afford a train ticket. She couldn't face their scorn and pity or her father's reminders that he had warned her of the consequences of a bad marriage, marrying "beneath her" as he always put it.

"What in the world are you complaining about? I give you a monthly allowance to run the house, don't I?

"It's not enough. It's nowhere nearly enough. Apart from food, I've got to stretch it to keep the two boys in shoes and clothes, never mind any clothes and toiletries for myself."

"You wear make-up too often anyway. Waste of money."

"It certainly is *not*. A woman must keep up appearances even in this dusty godforsaken town."

"It's a city. Regina is a city and the capital of the province."

"Capital of Hades as far as I'm concerned. If we moved to Vancouver my brother Bill could get you a job, a real job for real money."

"I don't want to move to Vancouver and I don't want to work for your brother. My job here pays well enough."

"Well enough for you to invest in that damn fool scheme of your friend Morrison to start a mink ranch."

"Disease. The mink got a disease. It would have made us rich."

"As rich as you got with stocks in that coal mine that ran out of coal? As rich as you got from stocks in that silver mine that never did have any silver? Your friend Brown would have drunk all the profits anyway before he skipped town, not that there were ever going to be two cents of profits."

"Harry Brown was a good guy. A lot of us believed in him. Just plain bad luck, that's all."

"I keep telling you, Lorne, it's not luck that makes you rich. It's hard work and thrift and good sense that makes people rich, but not overnight, no, not through hare-brained schemes."

"One of these days, Jean, one of these days …."

"Oh, surely, one of these days when pigs fly and roast pork is free. We need some more income, Lorne. I need more money to keep body and soul together. Soon. Do you think I want to have to go home to my parents and beg for help, for charity?"

"There's a depression on, did you notice? Times are tough."

"Of course I noticed. And I noticed that you came home late, again, reeking of beer."

"If you keep up this nagging, I'll be going back out."

"Oh, wonderful. Meet your responsibilities by walking away and heading back to the beer parlour. To spend money that you say you haven't got. Money for beer but not for your family. So, good, if that's what you want, if that's how you think, just go."

He slammed off into the hall and got his coat, then returned and said, "Divorce, maybe? Is that what *you* want, Jean?"

"Good Lord, no. You can't duck things that easily. Divorce, indeed! How could I face my friends? What could I say to our sons? How could I face my family, my parents, with that sort of stain on me? I'd be disgraced! How can you breathe the word 'divorce'? It's simply not done by respectable people."

He looked at her narrowly, growled "Oh, respectable", and then banged the door when he left.

Jamie turned on the light beside his bed and leaned across the small room to poke his older brother and wake him. Roy wasn't asleep either. The two boys looked at each other. Roy was stocky and dark, Jamie tall and skinny with light red hair. Both were upset.

"They've been fighting again, real bad."

"I heard."

"Why do they do it, Roy? It got pretty loud tonight. Why is it always about money that they fight? What do they need so much money for?"

"Well, I guess to buy things. To buy groceries and pay the rent and get coal for the furnace and stuff. And clothes, too, and bicycles. I keep telling Dad I need bigger skates because mine were biting my toes at the end of last season, but he just said maybe for Christmas."

"Do skates cost a lot?"

"Not a lot, I think, not if you buy them second hand."

"And you can buy clothes second hand, or so the guys at school tell me, but Mom says that's not a good thing to do. Degrading, she says, whatever that means."

"It means not nice, not good enough or something like that. There's lots of things you can't get second hand, she says, like pies or pencils for school or, I don't know, meat and other kinds of food. Expensive, she says, and cost money."

"And we don't have enough of it, is that it? Is that what they shout about?"

"Seem to be, yeh."

"It makes me worry, a lot of nights. Do you s'pose it's my fault, Roy?"

"Your fault? How could it be? Whatever put that idea into your head?"

"Well, I asked Mom if I could have a new bike a few days back. Maybe not a new one, but a used one. Mine is smaller than any of the other guys in my class, and I'm one of the tallest and my knees kinda go bonk, you know, on the handlebars. So maybe I shouldn't have asked if there's no money for it."

"No, no, don't talk crazy. We can always ask for things, that's OK, even if we know we're not likely to get them, not for a while, anyway."

"I hope you're right. I never meant to cause trouble. But I don't see how them fighting about it can get them more money."

"Can't, I expect, but Mom says cash is what makes the world go 'round. Makes people try to get better jobs or work harder so that they can buy more stuff, nicer things. People always try to get more money for themselves and more than other guys get. It's like when Dad gives us our allowance every week, if you got more than I did, or if I got more than you did, we'd probably get mad and fight about it, right? And that's what people do, they scrap, until they've got enough."

"How much would be enough, Roy, do you know?"

"Nope. It depends, I guess. On who wants what and how hard they're willing to work, or maybe how lucky they are, like being born rich, or getting away with stealing or finding a wallet on the street or winning prizes. Depends on lots of things. I remember I asked Uncle Milt about all this, and he laughed and explained it to me some, but I can't say I got it all clear. He said something about money not being very important or interesting once you've got enough, but he couldn't tell me how much enough is. Seems to me that enough might generally be a little more than we've got."

"You sure know a lot, Roy. I hope I know as much as you some day."

"Aw, I don't know much. I wish I did. It's just that I am five years older, that's all. But we can ask Uncle Milt to run through it all again sometime. For now, let's just go to sleep, eh? I've got a big game tomorrow. G'night."

Roy fell asleep almost immediately, but Jamie lay awake fretting for a long while. At about midnight he heard his father lurch in and utter a loud curse when he found Jean under a blanket in the living room, asleep on the couch.

III

Young Jamie McRae was full of misgivings and fears. He was much less sure of himself than his brother Roy who seemed to find everything clear and easy, brimming with self-confidence all the time. Jamie was more tentative. He worried about many things, some he could not bring himself to say out loud or discuss even with Roy. He leaned heavily on his older brother for advice and counsel, for help with his science homework and for explanations of things he didn't understand, like why their parents talked so little to each other except when they broke out into shrill slanging matches. Such outbursts disturbed him more than he wanted to admit and gave him a deep lifelong desire to avoid fighting of any kind. It was decades later before he understood that his was a normal reaction to growing up with a gruff and domineering father. We all try to evade situations we find upsetting. Jamie tended to hang back and observe and be cautious. This prompted his father to say, frequently, "The boy is too timid." Or "Dammit, I've got a creampuff for a son." Jamie didn't feel this was right or fair, but he was afraid that it might be.

One of his earliest fears was of death. His parents, lacking a babysitter, had taken him at age three-and-a-half or four to the funeral of a cousin in Lumsden, a cousin he'd liked, and the grey waxy face of the remains staring up from the coffin sent a freezing shudder up his spine. He'd asked his mother why cousin Donald looked so strange and didn't get up. His mother merely said it was because he was dead. To the question of whether the doctor couldn't make Don better the only reply was that being dead was final and forever, and hush, we must be silent; his soul has gone to heaven. What's a soul, he wanted to know, and his mother whispered that the soul was that part of you between your ears that thinks and makes you what you are. At which point his father glared at him and told him to shut the hell up. He did, but still didn't feel one bit better, only rather dizzy, even when Roy smiled and put an arm around his shoulders.

And dizzy was what he felt another time on a family outing in another town, he couldn't remember where, when the four of them climbed to the top of a water tower. Puffs of a stiff breeze ruffled their hair. You could see how flat the ground was for miles around and where the wind was making little swirls of dust devils near a dry creek bed. Roy seemed to think it was exciting to be up so high and threw a green-and-white striped peppermint over the edge of the railing and watched it fall. Jamie told Roy not to lean so far out, the wind might topple him off. Then his father snorted, seeing Jamie edge back from the railing and, muttering something about no kid of mine should be a pussyfooter afraid of nothing at all, grabbed him by the back of the collar and by the back of his belt and held him out over the edge, dangling him in empty air. His mother turned and let out a piercing shriek and clutched her breast and fainted. Jamie opened his mouth to shout but no sound came out. His heart thudded like a trip hammer until his father laughed and pulled him back and set him on his feet. Never again could he look down from a high ledge or balcony without a twinge of fear twisting his groin, never again could he feel comfortable with heights. Or with his father.

Thinking back, he could always remember those early events that caused his irrational fits of dejection or panic, but recollections of the causes did little to quiet his skittish feelings of unease. That all those reactions were understandable did not make them less real, like his fear of drowning which had its origins in the green waters of Lake Katepwa in the Qu'Appelle Valley when he was six.

The family had rented a small house trailer and was camping near the beach for two weeks. His father had gone for the day to Melville to try to sell a tractor to a friend over a few drinks in the beer parlour, and Roy was across the lake visiting a friend's cottage. Jamie and his mother were sitting on a blanket on the beach in the late afternoon when she got up to leave. Couldn't he stay here in the sand a bit longer? No, not alone, Mom said, and she had to go back to the trailer to start preparing dinner. He pleaded and she smiled and said she'd come back for him in fifteen minutes if he promised not to go into the water alone. He nodded but kept two fingers crossed behind him so that it wasn't a real promise, for he loved splashing about in the lake.

When he looked around and eyed the water he saw that most of the people had left the beach, no one on the little kids' water slide or the higher slide, no one beyond on the diving raft with its springboard, and he wanted to dive like the other kids. He couldn't swim, except for a bit underwater, but he was pretty sure the raft was in close enough to shore to walk to on tiptoes. He'd give it a try. The raft was anchored to a long chain and had drifted out further than it had been in yesterday's on-shore breeze, although he didn't realize that. When he had waded out up to his chin he was still about seven feet from the raft but, stubborn and determined, he bobbed along on his toes for another two feet and ducked under the surface to try swimming the rest of the way under water. It didn't work. He came up gasping and gulping, got a bad mouthful, began to choke, and realized he was in trouble. An attempt to let himself sink to the lake floor and then bounce up above the waves for air failed; he couldn't propel himself high enough to breathe air instead of water. He tried to turn and swim underwater back toward the beach but that didn't work either and, trying desperately to hold his breath, found he had no breath to hold. Another attempt to get his head high enough above the waves to shout for help resulted only in swallowing more water. Terror.

Two teenage boys on the beach at that time were debating whether to have one last swim for the day. Nah, said one, I've had enough.

Come on, urged the other, I'll race you to that beer bottle bobbing out by the raft. They both bounded into the water and swam swiftly to what proved not to be a bottle at all but the red head of a small boy. They pulled him out of the waves and on to the raft, then hung him upside down by his heels and pounded his back until a great stream of lake water gushed out of him and he gagged and gasped and started to breathe again. It was hard to tell who was most shocked, the rescuers or the rescued. They blinked uncertainly at each other for a minute or two until they decided to hold the boy up between them and drag him back to shore. There they finally got him to say and point to where he lived. When they got him back to his mother and started to explain what had happened she became hysterical and clutched him and moaned over and over again, Oh my boy, oh my Jamie, oh my boy. The two lads were embarrassed and began to shuffle away, but she had them repeat their story. Finally she got Jamie to say what he had done and how he had done it and how he was sorry, real sorry, that he had caused trouble. His mother sobbed profuse thanks to the teenagers and offered them money for what they had done, anything, what could she do for them? What we'd like, said one, if you've got any, would be a beer each, and laughed nervously. Although it crossed her mind that they probably weren't of age to drink she pulled herself together and gave them each two bottles of Drewry's Pale Ale from the ice chest.

At his mother's prompting Jamie told his version of the incident over again, more slowly, and she veered from wanting to scold him to needing to hug him and praise the Lord that he was safe. He didn't know how to say it or didn't want to say it, yet he still had a clear vision of his most panicked moments when he was afraid he was a goner and thought that he saw himself looking down from above at his own gasping, regurgitating body, with some kind of a white light gleaming at the end of a watery tunnel. Could he really have seen that?

His mother couldn't bring herself to scold him further. She did, however, launch into a lecture that puzzled him more.

"You've been spared for a reason," she said. "Never forget that you are a Milton. A Milton! Descended from the great poet with superior blood in your veins. You are doubtless destined for great things, I just know it. Foolish as you may have been, it's clear that God intervened and is looking after you and saved you for important purposes. With your heritage and God's grace it's certain that you'll grow up to be a fine man and accomplish great things. That is your destiny. I'm certain of it. Never forget, Jamie, that you are a Milton."

That didn't make a lot of sense to him, but he said only, "Yes'm," and was relieved that he wasn't going to be punished for disobeying about swimming.

When his father came home he sat listening rather stoically to the story and to his wife's loud wailing about what she kept calling "a brush with death", "a near tragedy". So far as Lorne could tell, Jamie had done a dumb thing and had ignored his mother's wishes, but whatthehell, was now safe and sound and quietly eating his dinner. Finally Lorne said, "All right, all right, all's well that ends well, so let's forget about it. If Roy had been there Jamie would have been okay. Too bad nobody on the beach had a camera so we could see what happened and maybe recognize the other boys. Oh well. Don't let's be so damn dramatic."

"Is that all you can say? Dramatic? A camera? We nearly lost a child, he was nearly drowned, and you can talk about a camera?"

"What do you want me to say?"

"Something, anything, but not about taking pictures!"

The father sighed and reached for his evening *Regina Leader-Post*. "Probably served him right, taught him a lesson. Damn fool kid. And who the hell has been taking my beer out of the ice chest?"

I V

At the beginning of the school year in 1939 when Jamie was almost seven his mother introduced him at tea to a family who had just moved into a very small house, almost at the end of their street down by Wascana creek. The family had a son named Mike who was quite small and shy and also six years old. Jamie was told that the next day he was to walk to school with Mike and show him around.

Mike remained silent during most of the walk until unexpectedly he burst out, "We had two meals yesterday!"

"Huh? How many do you usually have?"

"Just one. Oh, some bread or wheat porridge in the morning of course, which doesn't count, and then a hot supper at night, but yesterday we even had lunch too. Meat sandwiches made from a can of 'Spam' it was called. Do you and your folks have lunch?"

"I guess we do, yeh."

"And today my mom gave me this jam sandwich to bring to school, see?"

"Yeh, good. We live closer to the school so generally I go home for lunch. But you can have this apple I got, if you like."

"Could I have half of it?"

"Nah, take the whole thing."

"Gee, thanks a lot, Jamie, you're a real pal."

That evening Jamie asked Roy if he knew why people skipped lunch. His older brother told him it must be that thing about money again, something about the depression, but he didn't think he could explain what 'depression' meant except that a lot of people lost jobs and got poor. Roy said they'd ask their Dad about it at dinner. When they did, the only answer they got, apart from a grumpy scowl, was: "Ask your uncle Milt about that. He knows everything, at least he thinks he does."

When Milt came to their house on Sunday for dinner the boys took him out to the back porch and sat on the steps in the evening to put their questions to him.

Their uncle was, as usual, amused by their earnestness. A bachelor with no children of his own, he doted on them and brought them treats or presents even if there was no birthday or special occasion. Often he brought them books, knowing how bright they were. This evening he'd brought a book by Kipling and Hershey bars which they nibbled slowly to make them last longer.

Uncle Milt was Jean's favourite cousin. They'd grown up together in Calgary, were the same age and shared a strong emotional bond, not least because their mothers were friends as well as sisters. Tall, six foot two, dapper and lean, with a high forehead and a craggy face, Milt's hair was also prematurely white like his cousin's. He'd trained as a lawyer and kept some practice with paying clients even through the depression, working mainly for the provincial government on land and mortgage cases. At the end of the booming '20s he had made money on buying and selling real estate and was very comfortably off, continuing during the '30s to buy farm land at sacrifice prices or merely taking ownership by buying up properties for back taxes owed to the municipality, although he made a habit of letting the former owners continue to work and occupy the farms on a partnership basis if they wanted to. His reputation for shrewdness was enhanced by his standing in sporting circles. A fast and flamboyant left winger in hockey, a star wide receiver in football, he'd decided at the end of university not to pursue a professional career in athletics but to concentrate whole-heartedly on law. His full name, Chandler Preston Milton, seemed a bit unwieldy. As a nickname 'Chan' didn't please him when he was a boy, particularly when some of the kids took to calling him 'Charlie Chan' before he knocked the stuffing out of them. He became known solely as Milt, although when in the '30s he had more time on his hands and took the job of coaching the Regina Rangers junior hockey team with notable success, the local newspaper began to refer to him as 'The Silver Fox', a name which amused and secretly pleased him.

"So you boys want me to talk about money and the depression, is that it?"

"Yes please," said Jamie, "we asked Dad, and he said to ask you because you know everything."

"I'll just bet he did," Milt sighed, and Roy smiled, knowing full well the frequent tension between his father and Uncle Milt.

"It's a complicated subject. I'll try to keep it as simple as I can. I'd say money is like air, you never think about it as long as you're breathing, but if you run out of air you gasp and choke and die because you've gotta have it, or else. Let's see. You lads know the old saying, you never miss the water till the well runs dry? Money is like that. Money is what keeps you eating and drinking until it runs out. A depression is when most of the wells run dry. People are thrown out of work, they haven't got jobs to make money and they can't find any new jobs. No work, no money, you see?

"But this sort of depression is worse for us here on the prairies because of drought, lack of rain and water, so the farmers can't grow crops, and if they do manage to harvest a very small crop that the grasshoppers don't get, they can't sell their wheat for any kind of a decent price because there's no money around to buy it. So the farmers go broke and lose their farms, go bankrupt. When farmers have no money then everything stops around here, falls apart, and you've got yourself one helluva depression."

"When will things get better?" Roy asked. "Will it ever end?"

"It will end, so far as I can figure, when a war breaks out—mark my words there's a war coming very soon—and we'll spend millions, hundreds of millions, on guns and tanks and explosives to kill each other. People without jobs will become soldiers, older people without jobs will be put to work making war material, and they'll all get paid by the government, so they'll have money in their pockets and they'll want to spend it, so dollars will circulate all around and we'll have what they call 'prosperity'. The depression will be over."

"What about the farmers?" Jamie wanted to know. "Will they get their farms back?"

"Most of them won't, no, unless Mother Nature helps with huge rains and they learn to get together and help each other. That will take organization and a change of thinking, maybe a new kind of government."

"I don't rightly see," said Roy, "why the government, if it can raise money and spend millions and millions for an army, couldn't have taken those millions and spent them on the farmers and the workers who needed it in the first place."

"Ah, you've got one whup-doozer of a question there, Roy, with that good head on your shoulders. But that's a question I can't answer. Maybe nobody can. A real puzzler to everybody, certainly to me. And then we've got Jamie's little friend Mike and his family, there's an example closer to home."

"Mike seems very nice," said Jamie. "If his family hasn't got much food, would it be right to try to help them?"

"Of course, certainly, all we can. Mike's father is somebody I've known for years. Used to do a little legal work for him over a petty swindle by a grain elevator company. Got it settled out of court. The family is called Shevchenko and I sent Mike's mother to Jean when they gave up the farm and came to town. The father, Dan, is a very decent sort and I was able to find him a part-time job in a warehouse. He's also getting some work as a handyman, mostly carpentry, so I think his family is getting back on its feet. They won't be eating steak for a while yet, though, and my worry is that soon he'll have to join the army, maybe go off and get himself killed in the next bloody war."

"I don't like fighting," said Jamie. "It makes me sad."

"Me, too," said Milt, "although I guess there are some things you've got to fight for."

"Like what?" Roy asked.

"Like justice, I suppose, or like what you believe in."

"But not just to beat the other guy up?"

"No, nothing like that. Hey, now, haven't we been talking long enough? I don't want to bore you fellas. Your Dad says I talk too much. Wanna go in?"

"We don't get tired talking to you, Uncle Milt, we sure don't," Roy said. "What you told us about the depression helped a lot, even if I don't think I'll ever understand it all. Maybe you could say some more about getting jobs and like that. Could I get a job for money?"

"Oh, you're still too young for that, and your family feeds you pretty well, I'd say, better than most. But I suppose I could say more, yeh. It's certainly on my mind." Milt paused and drew out a cigar and lighted it. "The well has sure run dry for a lot of people.

"For example, a friend of mine told me just recently about one of his daughters, not a lot older than you, Roy, getting a job in a fruit and vegetable store. The pay was ten cents an hour, twelve hours a day, six days a week, and she came home thinking she was very lucky and told her family. Trouble was, when she showed up for work the next day her older sister had taken the job away from her by offering to work for eight cents an hour."

"That's mean," exclaimed Jamie.

"Damn right it is, but a lot of folks get real mean when times are tough." Milt puffed reflectively on his cigar. "And I was thinking, too, of the Shevchenko family we'd talked about. Their farm was down near Weyburn, desperately dry country in the heart of the dust bowl, and I was visiting with them, trying to help sort out some of their debts, for no fee of course, but I wasn't much use, because they lost the farm and went belly up."

"Couldn't they sell the farm for money?" Roy wondered.

"Nope. No buyers, and they already owed back taxes. But what busted them was debts for health care. You see, their Grampa got a terrible sickness, cancer, and he was in hospital a long time. He died there. That cost money, a lot of money, which they didn't have. The banks said no to a second mortgage on their land, and then there were the doctors' bills which they couldn't pay either. Flat broke. They are very solid people, and kind, even insisted that I stay to supper with them. I couldn't say no. 'Just pot luck,' they said, 'it won't be much' and it sure wasn't. In Weyburn you could buy a whole chicken for twenty or twenty-five cents, half a side of a pig for three or four dollars, and do you know what they had for dinner? Some bread made from old frozen wheat crushed up in a grinder, and stew. It was gopher stew. Not a great favourite of mine, but all they had to share."

When he paused to reflect on that, Roy said, "Wait. I've heard that hospitals have charity wards where you can go for free, Mom told me that happens. Couldn't their Grampa do that?"

"Afraid not. Even hospitals can't operate without money, particularly the smaller rural ones which can't run on credit. They've got to pay their nurses, if only twenty-five dollars a month, and buy medicine and meet their bills for heat and light and cleaners. So the Shevchenkos paid what they could, paid everything they could and finally had to give up, bankrupt. Their kids had no shoes. I felt very bad about it. They were proud people, who wouldn't accept any money or loan from me, and tried real hard till the end. Anyway, I was saying, after our meal of gopher stew, they invited me to come with them to a meeting in the schoolhouse, a political meeting. I wasn't keen on that, but they said the speaker was one of the best they'd ever heard, a real spellbinder, and you know how I feel about good talkers, so I went along. It was the cheapest entertainment around. This fellow had been elected to the parliament in Ottawa as a maverick socialist for a little party, the CCF. Name of

Douglas, T. C. Douglas, but everyone called him Tommy. Likeable guy. Small, like a bantam rooster and cocky, glinting glasses in the lantern light—there was no electricity, of course—big flashing smile. He is a Baptist minister, and I'm not generally a big fan of preachers, but oh golly could he speak! Wit, timing, cadence, a clipped and confident delivery. I was fascinated."

"What was he talking about?" asked Roy.

"That's the thing. He was talking about finding work for people. He said that in the southeastern part of the province there are millions of tons of lignite coal, mostly on Crown land—which means public land—that could be used to generate electricity. A dam on the Souris River would provide water for cooling turbines, and you could not only create jobs but produce enough power to bring electricity to thousands of farm homes, give them light and later refrigerators and hot water. One big burly guy, maybe two hundred forty pounds of him, heaved his bulk out of one of those little school seats and stomped to the door and turned and shouted, 'You're nuts!' But when I thought about it, I didn't think that preacher was nuts at all. Another fellow sitting near me muttered that Douglas must be a communist, but how could a Baptist minister be a communist? Near as I could tell, he was arguing that a democratic government should use its power to help people, not to leave them without electricity or jobs. Sure beats me to find much wrong with that."

"Do the Shevchenkos know this man, and like him?" Jamie wondered.

"They do, they like him a whole lot. Mainly they agree with him about public health insurance, to provide money for hospitals and health care that they couldn't afford. Douglas said he had made up his mind, years ago, that every citizen should have a guarantee of available health care, as a right, and that he'd do everything in his power to break down the money barriers between the healthcare system and those who needed it, so that people like the Shevchenkos wouldn't lose their homes and their farms to pay for doctors and medicine, or go without."

"Maybe you could explain, Uncle Milt, what 'insurance' is," said Roy. "I have some idea, but … How does it work?"

"Ah, lads, I'll try to do that," said Milt, stubbing out his cigar, "but not tonight. That's another big topic for another time, and I must be shoving along. I'll tell you, though, that after I did some court business in Weyburn, the next day I drove back out to the Shevchenko farm to say goodbye while they were packing up to move. I drove for a while through a dust storm, with Russian thistle tumbleweeds blowing into my windshield, and then the wind let up suddenly. I thought I saw some clouds in the west that looked like rain clouds, and when I got to their place I asked Dan whether he'd got a bit of rain. 'No, Mr. Milt, none at all. You've got to remember it's been seven years since we seen any real rain in these parts. Walter Sykes, now, just east of here, you know him? Well, just last week he got five drops of rain in his yard, five drops. One of those drops hit him square on the forehead and he was so amazed that he fainted dead away, unconscious. We had to throw three pails of dust on him to bring him to."

Milt chuckled at the memory. "Even in despair these men could find some laughter and hope. That's what I call real courage. Come to think of it, Dan told me repeatedly that what this fellow Douglas was offering was mainly hope. The message he got, Dan said, was that it's possible, it can be better, if the community pulls together we can make things better. I damn well like to think he's right. Without that hope, I guess, we might as well roll over and give the land back to the gophers."

V

One of the pleasures the two boys had was listening to the radio, something they often did together. Some evenings they'd sit on the floor in front of the RCA Victor upright console in the living room and stare at it raptly as they tuned in *Amos and Andy* or *The Lone Ranger* or *The Shadow*, *Fibber McGee and Molly* or *Lux Presents Hollywood*. They liked *Abie's Irish Rose*, although that was not permitted if their father was home because he disapproved of programs about "yids".

At lunchtime Jamie ran home real fast to hear *Lum 'n' Abner* and thought they were very funny. His father was almost always home for lunch too, but he said *Lum 'n' Abner* were "ignorant yokels", not to be bothered with. Lorne sat on the living room rug with his legs splayed and impassively played solitaire, seldom speaking, pausing in the flip of his cards only to roll a cigarette from Ogden's Fine Cut tobacco and smoking it absent-mindedly till mother said their sandwiches were ready. Jamie liked peanut butter sandwiches best, and often asked his mother for an extra half of one which he slipped into a pocket to take back to school in case his friend Mike didn't have enough.

One noon hour the radio announcer on CKCK Regina said that coming up was a song by a woman he knew his mother liked; Jamie called her from the kitchen. "Dinah Shore is in town and she's gonna sing!" His mother, brushing breadcrumbs from her shapeless grey housedress, came to listen but explained that it was not Dinah but a record, didn't he know that? At age seven it was the first he'd heard about records. There was no music in their house except the radio. It was some years later that Dinah Shore sang a catchy tune called 'Personality'.

And think of all those books about DuBarry's looks,

No doubt it must have been easy to see

The Madame had the cutest –

Personality.

It puzzled Jamie that his mother said she was "disappointed" in Dinah, and that the words were "vulgar and suggestive," whatever that was supposed to mean.

Late at night the boys listened to a small box radio, little more than a crystal set, that Roy had bought with money earned by shovelling snow. He'd strung a wire from it, out the bedroom window to the roof to serve as an aerial and on clear winter nights they could sometimes bring in stations as far away as Chicago. A lot of the American programs played jazz late at night on weekends and they listened to Paul Whiteman's orchestra, Artie Shaw, Tommy Dorsey, Glen Miller, and Benny Goodman, their favourite, particularly when Benny had Gene Krupa and Harry James with him. One of Roy's older friends told him that there was a coloured band, negroes, led by Chick Webb that 'cut' even Goodman, which they found hard to believe.

On Saturday afternoons in the autumn they listened to U. S. college football games and moved a cutout small paper football over a cardboard replica of a playing field to better follow the action. They liked the bands that played spirited college songs like "On Wisconsin" and the Notre Dame "Fight Song," Notre Dame being one of the teams they followed most closely because they'd read a magazine article in the barber shop about Knute Rockne and the Four Horsemen, a dynamite backfield. Their father, however, scoffed and pointed out that Notre Dame was Catholic school, a 'bunch of Doagans". "You mean, Catholic like our separate schools?" Jamie asked, and was rewarded with a grumble about being a "stupid kid".

"I didn't know they were Catholic either," Roy lied, "not that I see how it matters."

"Maybe I am dumb, but I sure try not to be. Seems to just be no pleasing our Dad sometimes."

"Dumb you aren't, pal. You know and I know you're the smartest kid in your grade at school. Mom knows it, too, even if Dad doesn't always remember. You're a great little guy and I'm proud of you. Dad's proud of you, too, it's just that he sometimes has a backhanded way of showing it. Maybe he has trouble letting his feelings out," said Roy, taking a precocious stab at psychological insight; "maybe he has problems of his own. I mean, parents must have some problems and hang-ups just like us, don't you think? Who's perfect, anyway?"

"I never thought of it like that. You sure know a lot, Roy. What sort of problems, do you think?"

"Oh, I wouldn't know that," Roy lied again, "there's no telling about parents, I'd say. Anyway, come on, let's knock it off and go out and throw the ball around. I'll be Jim Thorpe and you can be Slingin' Sammy Baugh, okay?"

Later on their addiction to radio raised another issue. The Canadian Broadcasting Corporation, the CBC, had a transmission tower at Watrous in the center of southern Saskatchewan between Regina and Saskatoon, its signal blanketing most of the province's population. A public broadcaster, a crown corporation and therefore carrying no commercials, it featured *Hockey Night in Canada*, from Maple Leaf Gardens in Toronto, with Foster Hewitt and the Hot Stove League. Hockey was okay with their father, but he objected to the boys listening to other CBC weekday programming such as the national news and dramas, and the Saturday afternoon music from the Metropolitan Opera in New York which their mother liked. The CBC, their Dad said, stood for Commie Broadcasting Corporation, programming by "pinkos" for eggheads and queers, not for "real" people. Why should his tax money go to support such junk, he often wondered aloud, and stomped out of the room when his wife tuned it in.

Puzzled about why this could cause conflict, Roy asked his favourite teacher in grade 9, Freddy Howarth who taught English, whether there was any problem with listening to the CBC. Mr. Howarth told him that in Britain and in most of Europe and the rest of the world public radio was "the norm", since governments of all stripes had decided in the '20s that radio was too powerful a medium to be left in the hands of pitchmen for soap and cars, and commercial broadcasting was not allowed. Canada did allow, he pointed out, some mix of commercial and non-commercial stations, but only the CBC had a national network. In the United States, however, public broadcasting was an extremely small part of the picture with private commercial stations and big business networks totally dominant, which seemed to Howarth an odd and unfortunate situation. "Unless you like your programs constantly interrupted by sales noises for cigarettes and deodorants." Often what seemed normal in the U.S. was considered abnormal almost everywhere else.

It wasn't that the CBC was created by "leftists", Howarth continued, but by the Conservative government of R. B. Bennett in 1933. Advised by a Royal Commission study, Bennett concluded that Canada should follow the British model, the public BBC, in order to provide radio service and educational programmes to rural and northern areas, neglected by private broadcasters, and to offset the intrusion of American networks. Bennett insisted that this was not so much a choice between state enterprise and private enterprise, but a pro-Canadian choice between "the state and the United States". Roy would find, said his English teacher, that the CBC provided higher quality listening and give him a feeling of being linked to the big outside world and its values beyond the borders of Saskatchewan.

The reason he wanted to explain all this, Howarth said, was that Roy should make a point of listening to some non-hit-parade music, classical music, which only the CBC carried. He also asked Roy to make a note of the day and time next week when CBK Watrous would be offering a performance of Hamlet, because that play would be on the English curriculum next year. Roy thanked him and promised to give it a try.

At the appointed time, just before Hamlet came on, their mother made it clear that she intended to sit in the living room with the boys and listen to it. This caused a loud and door-slamming exit by their Dad who proclaimed that he couldn't stand such nonsense, "long hair trash". "Bad enough I had to read such crap in high school. That bloody Shakespeare never said anything to me." He bellowed that he was going to the hotel, which meant to the beer parlour. Jamie began to see how important drinking was to his father, although Roy had known it for years. Beer seemed to fuel a lot of bitter and frightening arguments between his parents.

It was a popular ditty on CKCK that underlined, two weeks later, this domestic kerfuffle. Jamie and his friend Mike were playing Parchesi in the living room after school when the announcer said that the next song he'd play, after the commercial, would be 'Behind those Swinging Doors", and Mike said that his mother called that record 'the theme song of Mrs. McRae', so Jamie listened carefully. His mother overheard them from the kitchen and also paid attention.

> *The doors swing in and the doors swing out,*
> *As some pass in and others pass out.*
> *Your father I fear has his nose in the beer,*
> *Behind those swingin' in doors, those doors,*
> *Behind those swingin' in doors.*

Jean McRae wished she hadn't heard that. She dropped a cooking pot to the floor with a loud clatter. Her eyes misted over. She felt defeated, humiliated. It was unlikely that she'd ever be able to face Mrs. Shevchenko again. Maybe it was just as well that the lease on this rented house was almost up and that the McRaes would soon be moving for the second time in three years.

VI

All she wanted was a house. Apart from Roy and Jamie, that was what she cared about most. It didn't have to be large, just a place they owned, not rented, with a garden where she could plant flowers, and a fireplace. Her father's house always had a fireplace, which made all the difference between a house and a home. Surely that was not too much to ask? But all her married life she and Lorne had lived in rented bungalows, usually small and plain, ill-kept and needing paint, and none had a fireplace. Moving so often, and they were about to move for the sixth time, made her feel adrift and rootless, pushed from pillar to post. What was the point of planting tulips or making new curtains or sewing up old ones to almost fit new windows when she knew that within a year or two they'd be moving again to another drab and rundown bungalow? It was difficult enough to raise a family without having to worry about shifting the boys to different schools so often and feeling that the family had no stable foundation.

Just a house of their own. Every time they moved she'd tell her new neighbours that they were renting "only until they found just the right house to buy." She wanted to believe that, and sometimes she could almost persuade herself that it was true, would be true. The absence of hope can be a terrible thing.

Every time they moved she'd tell her father in Calgary that her new address was "probably just temporary". Too often, it was. Her brother in Vancouver tried to lighten her spirits over the phone by joking that "she has a well-travelled family". She tried to conjure up a laugh, but couldn't. Travel was another painful subject. She's always hoped to be able to see Europe one day, but that was now far beyond her most extravagant dreams.

Canada's declaration of war against Germany in September 1939 changed a lot of things. Whereas there had been no jobs for the thousands of unemployed, now there were jobs, either carrying guns or making guns. Ironically there was full employment, just as Uncle Milt had predicted. Oliver Farm Equipment, like many industrial firms, announced that it was switching to war production and began to lay off field staff. There were no tractors for salesmen to sell. Lorne McRae was among those let go.

For a few days after he was fired, without benefits or severance pay, Lorne continued to leave the house at eight in the morning in his shiny brown suit and tie, pretending to be going to the office, trying to conceal the fact of his unemployment. He told his wife that the company car, which had been taken back, had gone into the shop for a complete engine overhaul that might take quite a while. He spent most of each morning walking, aimless and disconsolate, cursing his luck. When his feet became too tired and sore he would sit on a bench in a secluded south corner of Victoria Park, hoping not to see anyone he knew. Afternoons he'd skip lunch and go directly to the Hotel Saskatchewan beer parlour to drink slowly but steadily from glasses of ten-cent draught lager. Sometimes he'd eat a pickled egg from the big jar on the bar, but food interested him less and less. The beer, however, was making him pudgy and his belly was becoming distended.

Normally he went home about seven-thirty to a frosty reception from Jean. "Had to entertain a customer from out of town," he'd say, "a customer wanting to buy some second-hand machinery." Lorne was well known and quite popular in the beer parlour because he was a man's man, cordial and a good listener with his fellows, interested in sports and in politics. Two of his best friends, Davey Morrison and Lyle Gardiner, occasionally dropped by to share a few draughts with him between five-thirty and seven; both were white collar small businessmen who liked a glass or two but not more, and both were strong supporters, like Lorne, of the governing Liberal party. All three were glad that the depression seemed to be lifting and that there'd be no more trouble with those damned socialists.

After a few weeks of walking and worrying and hard drinking he was driven to search for work. He was broke. Trying to raise cash from his considerable holdings of speculative penny stocks netted him, after broker's fees, a total of seventy-eight dollars, not enough to go far or to placate his increasingly clamorous wife.

Lyle told him of a business acquaintance in his Rotary Club who might be hiring staff and arranged an introduction. Soon Lorne, in his best blue suit and a red tie and polished shoes, was interviewed and hired by Mac Kendall of Kendall Van Lines as an assistant manager with, once again, a company car, Mac's own old used 1937 Buick sedan, black, with side mounts. Roy and Jamie thought it was the grandest car they'd ever ridden in, and even their mother took some pleasure in it. She loved to go for drives on Sunday afternoons. Dad wanted to drive out into the country as far as Lumsden in the Valley, while Mom wanted to go up and down the streets in the affluent Lakeview area near man-made Wascana Lake in front of the legislative buildings, just to look at the big houses there. They reminded her of her father's house when she was a girl, and now stood as a rebuke that she didn't have one and probably never would, but still she wanted to drive by them. The two boys didn't much care where they went as long as they could stop for ice cream cones.

Some Sundays they drove as far Moose Jaw, forty-five miles away, where they'd swim in the spring-fed mineral pool of the Natatorium and share various dishes of Chinese food at the Exchange Café. Until after the war the road between Moose Jaw and Regina was the only paved road in the province, all other roads including the Number One highway in the province being gravel. Frost upheavals and drainage problems caused the road surface to deteriorate during wartime neglect and made driving rough and jolting, threatening the springs and shock absorbers of the Buick. By 1943 the Department of Highways decided to put up a sign at both ends of the road: Watch Out for Breaks in the Pavement. Some wag blacked out several words with paint so that it read: Watch Out for the Pavement. Soon the family found it more prudent to avoid that road entirely.

It seemed the family fortunes might be taking another turn for the better when the manager of Kendall's, a man younger than Lorne who had been with the company six years, got a hernia fixed and was accepted into the air force as a gunner. This meant Lorne was promoted to manager at least till the end of the war. In essence he was still a salesman. An accountant ran the office while he called on companies that were transferring executives into or out of the city and would examine their furniture to give written estimates of what the packing and moving would cost. Local moves within the city were also an important part of the business, but short hauls were less profitable. With so many people moving around during the war it was a flourishing business.

Jean became encouraged by her husband's improved salary and began to press again for buying a house. To buy penny stocks could be only squandering money on idiotic gambling, she said, while a house was an investment. Paying rent meant that you'd never see that money again, but a purchase of real estate would build equity and help stabilize the family. That might well be true, Lorne agreed, if he had a chunk of savings for at least a twenty per cent down payment, and that's what he didn't have. If she was so damned keen to buy a house why didn't she ask her family in Calgary or cousin Milt for a loan, or what he called "bridge financing". Jean was, of course, too ashamed to ask for anything like that. The usual result of those disputes was more arguing and fighting between the parents, frequently late at night, frequently noisy and acrimonious. Sometimes when Roy woke up early he found his mother sleeping on the couch and he'd tuck in her blanket, but it didn't seem to him right. At least they are shouting more about money and less about drinking, he thought, although none of it ever seemed to get anywhere, and none of it made the home atmosphere more relaxed or cheerful.

Dinnertime at the McRae's was often strained. One evening they were having their usual quiet meal, one of their frequent silent meals, finishing up wieners and beans before Jean served apple cobbler for dessert. Jamie, feeling uneasy in the hushed tension, suddenly heard himself noisily break wind. Roy grinned at him; their Dad didn't even look up from his plate. Jamie looked sheepishly at his mother who exclaimed, "Oh, Jamie made a little breeze, a poopendooper. Maybe he should go toidy." She went twittering out to the kitchen for the cobbler.

"Toidy," Roy mumbled. "'Breeze'. Dear God."

Lorne shook his head. "Your mother couldn't bring herself to say 'fart' if one blew her into the next room. Much too refined. Drives me nuts."

Roy nodded. He'd long ago recognized that certain things were simply not to be said. To his mother, a roasting chicken didn't have a 'breast', merely a 'front part', and the rear end was either 'the pope's nose' or 'the part that goes over the fence last'.

His father continued: "She's a bit batty, you know, and on certain subjects she makes no sense at all for a grown woman. Means well, I guess, but …. Is she still harping on that 'always remember you're a Milton' crap?"

"Well, yeh, sometimes."

"Pay no attention to that. Some goddam Limey poet, is all. Just be grateful she doesn't believe she's descended from Queen Victoria or Carrie Nation."

Not sure who Carrie Nation was, Roy only nodded again. He couldn't remember his father ever stringing so many sentences together at one time, never mind saying critical things about their mom. He shot a quizzical glance at his dad.

"Still," said Lorne, "I suppose she's a good mother."

"Sure."

"At least, I hope she's a good mother to you boys. To me, she's not much of a ...." He sighed. "Oh, never mind. I'm talking too much. Forget I said anything at all, hear?"

"Uh hunh. I'm just sorry you and mom don't get along better."

"In some ways we do, son. Some ways." He avoided Roy's eyes. "It's, um, complicated. Maybe if I struck oil in the back garden and built her a mansion, she might be satisfied." He pushed up a mirthless laugh. "Now, where in hell has Jamie got to? You'd better fetch him if he's going to have any dessert. I might go out for a while."

Roy found his brother in the basement sitting on the floor in front of an open cardboard box.

"Look what I found. Come and take a look."

""What is it? Oh, photographs."

"Yeh, old ones. See, this is one of all of us that I remember from before the last time we moved. I wondered what became of it."

He passed over an enlarged snapshot of the four McRaes at the beach, lined up in a vertical row: Lorne standing at the back, Jean sitting on a beach ball in front of him, with her hands on the shoulders of Roy who was crouching, and Jamie sitting on the sand in front.

"I remember this," said Roy. "Mom liked it too. I think it was taken when we were at Katepwa in that trailer, the time you did that imitation of a beer bottle in the lake. You look so solemn, Jamie, worried, as though you had all the cares of the world on your head."

"Could be I thought I did."

"How many years ago was this?"

"Hm, about four or five, I guess. You look as though you were bursting with energy you might pop right out of the picture. Dad is looking up and away at the trees as if, I dunno, as if he'd rather be someplace else."

"What gets me is how much younger we all looked then, not just you and me, but mom in particular. We all change, eh? But mom was prettier then, big smile, bright-eyed and bushy tailed, with her hair up and all. She still has that outfit hanging up somewhere, red and white beach pajamas, but I don't remember her ever wearing them since. Don't you think she looks older now, after only a few years?"

"Yeh, now that you say it. Less, um, lively than in the picture. These days she looks more like what you said about me, worried, more sad. Less pep."

"Damn," said Roy, and shook his head. "Makes you think, doesn't it? Well, anyway, come on back upstairs and let's see if we can still get dessert."

Lorne, meanwhile, had gone out for a beer and sat casting about for ways to make extra money. He was impressed by how profitable the trucking business seemed. Kendall had become a rich man who spread his business interests into hotels and a dry cleaning chain. The more Lorne poured over the van line books the more he became convinced that he too could build a lucrative trucking company. The initial problem as always was lack of capital. After a lot of discussions of cost and revenue figures, and a lot of drinks in the beer parlour, he persuaded Davey Morrison to become his (silent) partner in the new venture. Morrison's money bought two used trucks in 1944, one small van for local moves, one long-box van for out of town hauls. A bank loan with the trucks as collateral yielded enough money to rent part of a small warehouse for storage, to paint the trucks orange and black with a big logo on the sides, and to hire two worker-drivers. McRae's Moving and Storage was born.

After the first few months the company was breaking even and after four months began to show a small profit. He began to brag to his friends in the beer parlour how simple it was to make money and become a successful businessman. Joining the Kiwanis Club brought him new contacts and prospective customers. He told his wife that they'd be able to buy a house within a year, maybe even with a fireplace if she insisted, and bought her a new winter coat while he was riding a crest of optimism and apparent affluence. Not at all lazy, he worked himself very hard and did a lot of the packing and furniture moving personally with his hired men, driving the bigger van quite often on long distance hauls. The demanding labour helped to slim him down, flatten his belly, and boost his confidence. Even Jean seemed happier as she handled the phone and kept the office running. She found it ironic that, having themselves moved so often, they should find themselves in the moving business, but it might work out after all, might be as easy as he said.

It wasn't. First Kendall and other truckers put the word around that McRae's was just a two-bit fly-by-night operation that was not reliable. Competitors began to undercut McRae's prices and out-bid him for large jobs. One of the trucks broke down and it took four long days to get it towed and a cracked motor block replaced. But delays and stiffer competition were not the worst of it.

That came in April with a long haul load to the west coast. Lorne was very happy that a fellow Kiwanian named Burton had engaged him to move his household to Vancouver and that promised to be a most profitable trip. He'd do the packing and drive the van himself. Roy could ride along to keep him company and to see the sights since he'd never been out of Saskatchewan. That sounded just great to Roy. Jamie envied his brother's good fortune though he tried to conceal his disappointment.

Packing furniture and household goods for a long haul is difficult; it can be very tricky to ensure that everything rides well and nothing gets scratched or broken. As he worked at it with a crew of two men and some help from Roy, Lorne slowly realized he'd have a problem fitting everything from the large house into a single load. Carefully he rearranged five mattresses and two big couches so that they touched the ceiling of the twenty-seven-foot truck box and altered the position of several other bulky items, but still it was a very tight fit. No matter how he arranged things it looked as though three assiduously packed wooden barrels—one of a Spode china table setting for eight, one of antique silver tea services and ornaments, one of crystal glassware, Dresden figurines and framed photographs—simply could not be crammed into the truck. Damn! What to do? Taking a second truck was out of the question; his other smaller and older van probably couldn't make it. Shipping the barrels separately by rail might take god knows how many more weeks and be an admission that he couldn't handle everything. Asking another van line to help him out would produce only scorn and laughter from his larger competitors. The horns of the dilemma were damnably sharp.

The only viable solution seemed a bit of a stretch. He'd close up the rear doors as usual, keep the four-foot tailgate down on its supporting chains, place the barrels on that platform, weld a retaining bar along the rear edge of the tailgate, and attach two broad heavy leather straps horizontally around the bellies of the barrels, bolted to the sides of the van. That seemed to work. It looked tight.

The early part of the trip and across Alberta went smoothly. The barrels were checked every hour or two and rode securely. Lorne relaxed and congratulated himself on how well he'd solved the problem. He decided not to take the main and more northerly route from Calgary to Revelstoke to Kamloops and down to Vancouver, but to keep to a smaller highway, B. C. #3 to the south from Lethbridge to Cranbrook and over to Trail, closer to the U. S. border. This more direct secondary route would save time and gas and money.

Roy thought the mountains were splendid. He hummed and whistled along the trip. Everything was fine and dandy until the morning of their third day out. They'd slept in a bed and breakfast in Trail and after toast and scrambled eggs were told in a gas station that the road west was "passable" after spring runoffs. From Trail to Rossland was easy and then they confronted what the map showed as a gravel road through the Christina mountain range and over the Cascade hump. Rough and bumpy and ungraded since winter, the road seemed little more than a narrow track, but they pushed on. At an altitude of about seven thousand feet with the motor labouring in third gear the truck jounced and shook as they drove slowly over some very pitted washboard surface that made everything vibrate. A mercifully flat spot a mile onward enabled Lorne to pull over and stop to check the rear load. Roy got out to pee. He heard his father emit a strange strangulated cry and rushed to the back of the van. Two of the three barrels were gone. Just gone. Their top lids had vibrated and jolted off and, without them, the staves had collapsed inward under the pressure of the tight leather straps, scattering the contents of the barrels along the road.

Roy knew better than to say anything. His father too said nothing. Lorne leaned against the tailgate for what seemed an endless two minutes of silence, then shuffled to the side of the road and threw up. He wiped his mouth, shook his head and spat. From his suitcase in the truck's cab he pulled out a micky of rye whiskey, drank a jolt of it. They re-secured the remaining barrel and turned the van around to drive slowly back toward the east in hopes of recovering some of the lost goods. All they found was a lot of broken china tangled in excelsior shred packing and a few battered photographs in bent frames, scattered over more than a mile of the gravel trail. Sadly the one intact barrel was the middle one containing the silver tea services, heavier objects which might have survived crashing to the road, but ....

During the remainder of the drive to Vancouver not much was said. They listened to the tinny truck radio and tried to enjoy the impressive mountain scenery, but both of them brooded over the bleak future of McRae's Moving and Storage. Several times his father darkly muttered, "insurance", so Roy tried to see some hope in that, although he knew that the owners of the load would be certain to raise merry old hell.

On arrival Lorne phoned the British Columbia office of his insurance company even before driving to Mr. Burton's new home in Burnaby to unload with the help of two workers hired for the day. The off-loading went briskly and without incident until Mrs. Burton, with a furrowed brow, began to question where, in which packing cases, she could find and check her Spode china? And the large collection of Dresden pieces? And where were the family photographs? Lorne insisted that two more barrels would soon arrive by rail, to be delivered by a CPR truck. Mrs. Burton was extremely surprised and agitated by that explanation. She phoned her husband and then the railroad company, but was not at all reassured, since the CPR didn't know what she was talking about. Lorne and the crew finished up hastily and were ready to drive away when Mr. Burton arrived, trying to mollify his wife and shouting what in the flaming hell was going on? Where were those barrels? Where was the railroad bill of lading? How could he hope his wife would calm down until she found her family photographs, the photos of her parents and her children? What in the name of Christ was this all about anyway?

Lorne decided to beat an ignominious retreat as fast as possible and got the van started. Burton left his wife's side and ran to his car to move it so that he could block the truck's departure, but he was a little too late. He stood on the sidewalk and bellowed and gesticulated wildly. Roy looked back at him in the side mirror and never forgot the sight. We're scuppered, he said over and over to himself, scuppered. Sonofabitch. He kept looking at his father who just set his jaw and wiped his brow and kept driving.

The next morning, after drinking many morose beers in their cheap hotel's men's beverage room, eating nothing and sleeping very little, Lorne drove to a trucking terminal and met with the insurance claims adjuster. The man listened to the story and asked a lot of questions. Were the barrels carried inside the van? Not exactly. Where, then? Well, on the tailgate, but secure. Had the barrels collapsed? No, no, certainly not collapsed. They had been stolen while the truck was parked overnight in Trail, B. C. Surely the insurance company covered theft. The man said no, not unless the items had been stolen from inside a locked van. Had all this been reported to the Trail police? Well, no, he'd been too distressed to think clearly and do that. But he would, he would do it now, by phone. Roy looked at his father with pity and shame and walked away. The insurance man closed his briefcase and said, no, there's no valid claim, as the policy clearly indicated. He shook his head and repeated, sorry, no claim, and advised Lorne to get out of town as quickly as possible before Mr. Burton decided to press legal charges of negligence or willful breach of contract or fraud.

During the long trip home Roy couldn't stop thinking, poor ol' dad, poor sad bugger. What awful rotten luck. Here's a man who tried so hard, wanted it so bad, but now ....

When they got back to Regina, the truck empty or "deadheading" with no return load, McRae's Moving and Storage was slapped with a huge lawsuit for loss and damages. The value of the family photographs was described as "inestimable". Lorne did the only thing he could do. He declared bankruptcy. Everything was lost. In the beer parlour he reflected on his colossal bad luck. At least he wouldn't lose his house, because he had no house to lose.

VII

The family knew that both boys were bright. Both were avid readers. Roy found math and science quite easy, and Jamie did better in English and history. Toward the end of the school year, Jamie's grade eight teacher sent a note home with him, sealed because it wasn't the school's policy to let students know such things, discussing the results of his IQ tests. Miss Perkins wrote that Jamie had scored quite high, above 130, and was certainly university material in the future, but she expressed puzzlement. His score would have been significantly higher if he'd "made any real attempt at the mathematics part of the test on which he achieved very few points."

His mother was not surprised but very pleased with this report. When she showed it to Lorne she cooed and crowed and repeated: "I kept telling you he was bright. He could go a long way. After all, he's a Milton." The father seemed unimpressed. "So the kid's got brains. Big deal. It's too bad he doesn't use them more often. And what's so great about all this 'language' and 'logical and conceptual skills' stuff if he can't add and subtract?"

While Roy was away for eight days on what later became known as "the barrel trip", Jamie was in low spirits. He acutely missed his big brother, protector and best friend. He'd never been parted from Roy before and began to realize more fully how dependant he was on the companionship, advice and support of the older boy. Jamie had other friends from school, but when Roy was away things just didn't feel the same.

Resigned to his father's rather remote dealings with him, and the sense that his father thought less of him than he thought of Roy, Jamie came to rely on his brother as a mentor as well as for a buoyant effect on his shifting emotional tides. He was convinced that Roy could do almost anything. Building model airplanes got easier when Roy showed him how, as did fixing a bike or building a birdhouse or learning how to throw a curve with a baseball. (A "hardball" they used to call it until they were abruptly told by the father that softball such as they played in grade school was a game for girls and not really baseball at all.)

Jamie tried, hard, but he knew he could never be the crack athlete that Roy was or measure up to the father's stern expectations. Roy was a fearless competitor, a terrier who would keep at it until he got it right, and once he'd sunk his teeth into a game he'd never let go whether his team was comfortably ahead or down by ten–nothing. Jamie was a faster runner than Roy, but never as fast a skater or as nifty a stick-handler in hockey, and lacked Roy's reckless abandon in wading into scraps and flattening people. It was years later before Jamie recognized that Roy was driven by pride and anger, anger at his own circumstances and particularly at his father. Jamie, on the other hand, tended to cheer for the underdog and feel sorry for people, for slower opponents in track and field, for his mother, and even for his father. Roy would slap him on the back and say that he was "all heart", but that games were a great outlet for pent up aggression and letting your emotions out, when you could bash somebody at the blue line on the ice or knock someone senseless on the football field and get praised for it rather than blamed or arrested.

Reading, more than sport, became Jamie's main pleasure. He'd much rather read about games than play them, particularly to read about baseball. He ransacked the public library for books about Ty Cobb and Roger Hornsby and Christy Mathewson, and when his mother sent him for a haircut he'd arrive early at the barber shop to pore over sports magazines and imagine what a wonderful world it would be to travel with teams as a sports writer, seeing his name in print as the author of a story about Babe Ruth. Later he'd remember Roy helping him to sneak in to the bleachers of Regina's rickety baseball "stadium" to see two barnstorming U. S. teams, the House of David, resplendent in beards, and the Harlem All Stars, led by the great Leroy "Satchel" Paige, a tall loose-limbed black man who moved with a slow elegance. They saw Satch well after his prime, although he still had wicked stuff. He threw an apparently effortless two-hitter against the Davids with a sweeping curve ball that looked as though it would be high and away and then break in toward the batter's ear. The newspaper reporter mentioned that Paige had lost a little off his fastball and dug out the old quote of Satch's that "If ah cain't out-push 'em, ah out-cutes 'em." Roy whooped with delight at that, and Jamie never forgot the line. "Brains can baffle brawn," said Roy. "Always remember that, little pal, and you'll do fine." Jamie was a lot more pleased with that comment than with the reaction of his father who called Satch "just a rubber-armed nigger freak." It's a sad thing to know your own father was a bigot. Jamie never forgot that line either.

Roy's absence gave Jamie more time to read. He read voraciously. He waded through a lot of pulp fiction magazines about aviation and sports and war. By the end of grade eight he'd moved on from *Dave Dawson in the R. A. F.*, Henty's *With Wolfe in Canada*, and the *Hardy Boys* mysteries to tackle Dickens, and instantly recognized an author who was playing in a higher league. His mother encouraged this pursuit and arranged to borrow a complete set of Dickens for the summer from Uncle Milt.

Lorne's reading was limited mainly to Zane Grey's westerns and Ellery Queen. Jean, having graduated from Teachers' College before she married, fancied herself an intellectual and read people like Willa Cather and Pearl S. Buck who didn't much interest the boys. D. H. Lawrence she considered "immoral and unsuitable", Aldous Huxley "dangerous and too modern", whatever that might mean. But one book she brought home from the library, having put in a reserve slip for it months in advance as one had to do with things on the best-seller list, was Lin Yutang's *The Importance of Living*, a jaunty popularized account of Chinese philosophy and wisdom. Roy read half of the book and was only mildly interested, and surprised that his kid brother found it so fascinating.

Jamie's more impressionable and romantic nature was captivated by the delicate sentiments of some of the Chinese writers presented in translation and the calm, detached view of life reflected by the sages, most particularly by the author's account of his own cheerful religious beliefs in a chapter titled 'Why I am a Pagan'. This reminded the boy of his own unsettling experience at age nine that gave him early doubts about orthodox Christianity.

His parents had sent him to the nearby Presbyterian Sunday school, clutching a dime for the collection plate, although they seldom if ever attended church themselves. Questions he put to the Sunday school teacher were what caused trouble. If God made the universe, Jamie wanted to know, who made God? It seemed a simple and obvious question. The answer that God was spirit and the Unmoved Mover didn't satisfy. How could a spirit create a tangible material world? Because God was all-powerful and could do anything. If he could do anything, why did he not deal with hunger and poverty and suffering? We must not question God or doubt that He is Good, God is Love. Then why does God permit war and the slaughter of the innocent? And if God's son was Jewish, why were Christians to mean and cruel to Jews? The ways of God can be mysterious, said the Sunday school teacher. I'd better arrange for you to have an interview with Reverend MacGregor who can explain much better.

The Reverend, however, was no more successful or persuasive than his delegate had been. Jamie was interested in dinosaurs, as many boys are, so if God made the world in six days, how come the dinosaurs walked the earth millions of years before people did? That's just another story that can be puzzling, allowed MacGregor, but perhaps each of

God's days was a million years, since God was eternal and timeless. Jamie only blinked at that. And how should he understand the virgin birth of Jesus; did virgins really have babies? The Reverend managed a thin smile and replied that there were some things he really couldn't discuss with a boy so young. He could only say that while Jamie was a bright lad, and an inquiring mind was acceptable to God, there were many mysteries that were difficult to explain and had to be accepted on faith.

When the interview was over Jamie had the feeling that the Reverend was as relieved as he was. He decided that he'd ask Uncle Milt about some of these things. Meanwhile, he'd drop out of Sunday school without telling his parents and spend his collection plate dime on chocolate ice cream. But he continued to wonder and worry about such things.

That was why three years later he was ready for Lin Yutang's guileless advice about being a pagan. At whatever age, you have to be ready for a book before its voice can really speak to you. Jamie felt liberated from the sour and repressive code of the Presbyterians (and later all Christians) who accepted the strictures of orthodoxy. Surely the theologians were the greatest enemies of the simple ethics of the early Christian gospels. Paganism could rescue religion from theology, or so he came to believe. It seemed to him that the Golden Rule of the Bible, followed to gain merit in heaven or to avoid the fires of hell, was no advance at all on the much earlier teaching of Confucius that the guiding rule should be 'Reciprocity' and that, with or without a God, we should lead decent lives simply because we are decent human beings. The concept of original sin, about which Jesus had never uttered a recorded word, struck the lad as a laughable priestly addendum. Jamie found he could live like a spiritual orphan, without any church or elaborate doctrine, sustained only by a reverent attitude toward nature, feelings of gratitude and awe in the midst of beauty and mystery.

Sometimes he wondered whether he and Dr. Lin Yutang were the only two people in the western world who understood all this. It all seemed so beguilingly simple. But then, young men are always looking for the simple, particularly during the turmoil of adolescence.

The other big issue he was eager to discuss with Roy when he got back from Vancouver was their neighbour, Mrs. Campbell. She was the brash wife of an older man who seemed always to be away on sales trips. He knew that Roy had taken a lot of notice of her, and agreed that it was hard not to. As Jamie's voice had changed and grown deeper, so did his interest in girls, but none of his awkward and flat-chested schoolmates could compare with the bounteous Chrissy Campbell. Slim, with a tiny waist and high full breasts, she jiggled when she walked, constantly brushing waves of unruly auburn hair out of her bright azure eyes. Although she seemed very old, say, 35, she behaved like a frisky young colt, sunbathing in her back yard in a skimpy yellow bathing suit or, even if she was walking only to the corner store, clicking down the street in high heels. Roy had whispered more than once, "get a load of those legs". Because he knew that Roy kept a well-thumbed copy of *Forever Amber* hidden in his closet and two copies of a nudist magazine, *Sunbathing*, secreted in a pile of old Captain Marvel comic books, Jamie was increasingly alert to what his brother meant by nudging him and saying "zowie" or even "hot stuff". Whether Chrissy Campbell was aware of the boys' lively admiration was uncertain, although Roy said he thought she'd winked at him at least once when she caught him staring. She's a real dish, he said.

The boys knew that their mother had firm views on their neighbour; she'd expressed them several times. "That woman is coarse," she'd said, "an over-painted hussy", and "a Jezebel". Gossip that Mrs. Campbell was a divorcee shocked Jean, but seemed to amuse Lorne. Mother had frowned at the expensive wispy underthings Mrs. Campbell hung outside on the line to dry—lingerie, she called it—while she herself was careful to dry her "unmentionables" on a clothes horse in the basement. Their father once muttered that the older the boys got the more things they'd find that their mother disapproved of. These strictures did nothing but quicken the boys' interest.

One morning Mrs. Campbell knocked on the McRae's door and inquired whether she might borrow a little of Roy's time to help her with a project. She wanted to knock down a bit of plastering, a partition arch between her dining and living rooms, and surprise her husband with the completed job. No, Roy was in Vancouver with his father "on a business trip", but perhaps young Jamie could help her? Yes, thank you, said Mrs. Campbell, and Jamie leapt at the chance.

It turned out that the neighbour was not entirely clear on how to go about the job but didn't lack confidence. She disappeared into the basement and re-emerged wearing tight slacks and a blue-checked man's shirt with the tails tied above her waist, showcasing her navel, and carrying a stepladder. Jamie was just to hold the ladder steady, please, while she climbed up with a hammer and chisel to make some exploratory taps. Maybe, Jamie suggested, if you've got a drill, Mrs. Campbell, we could drill a few small holes to see what's behind the plaster holding it up before you … ? Haven't got a drill and I don't see any need and call me Chrissy. I don't much like being called Mrs. Campbell. Yes'm. Yes, Chrissy. He liked the sound of that.

She continued to tap and then to pound on the chisel without noticeable effect except a few punctures along the line between the arch and the ceiling. Damn and blast, she muttered. Hand me that bigger hammer, would you? Yes, Chrissy. Thanks. Now I'll get serious with this damn plaster and show it who's boss. And she fetched it a vigorous blow and the chisel cut right through plaster and lathing and suddenly, smash, a whole section of the arch came apart and fell on her head.

This cascade prompted a small scream of surprise and dismay as well as a remarkably imaginative stream of cursing and invective such as he had never before heard from a woman. He was amazed. Covered in thick plaster dust, she leapt off the ladder and began to shake out her long hair, still swearing. Then she unbuttoned her shirt and shrugged it off and began to wipe her marvellous cleavage with it and tugged at her startlingly red lacey brassiere. Jamie was even more amazed. He eyes grew big as pie plates.

She looked up from her white dusty bosom and exclaimed, "Oh, sorry, Jamie, I wasn't thinking. You all right?"

He tried to say "yes'm", but no sound came out. His small but hard penis paid silent tribute to what he thought was the most impressive sight he had ever seen.

"Why, I do believe you've got an erection. Isn't that nice. Aren't you sweet. I wouldn't have thought …. How old are you, Jamie? Twelve?"

"Almost fifteen, Chrissy."

"Well well. Almost fifteen. That's a pretty big 'almost'. My my. Would you like me to do something about it?"

"Um, like what, Chrissy?"

"Well, like this," she laughed, reaching for his fly, "or maybe like this. I don't need a buttonhook to get this out. Does this feel better? I'll just bet it does, eh?"

"It's, it's …."

"Mustn't be shy. Boys shouldn't be shy."

"No, Chrissy."

"Now, would you like to take my brassiere off? That might be nicer for you, humm?"

"I … I don't know how."

"Oh, of course. Let me do it," she said, continuing to fondle him with one hand, reaching behind her with the other. "It comes off like this. There. Do you like them?"

He remained in a dazed speechlessness, too stupefied to reach or touch.

"You may touch them if you like. I'd like that, too. Yes. And then the next thing I want you to do …."

But by then it was too late. He shuddered and exploded. She assured him that was all right, that was fine, and if he came back to visit her again the next day there were some things she'd be happy to teach him.

All he could say was, "Really? Is there more?"

"There is more," she laughed. "Quite a bit more. But you must be sure not to mention all this to your mother, not to anyone, hear?"

He could only nod his assent and gratitude. The truth was he was still not clear if this was what was meant by "having sex", or if he'd done anything wrong, or whether he yet understood (as years later he read someone put it) who does what and with which and to whom. But he was desperately eager to learn.

He returned the next afternoon and his ecstatic tutorial continued. Lucky is the boy who is initiated by a generous older woman.

It was too good to last. His mother, having a vague intuition that something wasn't quite right, forbade him to visit their neighbour any more, renovation or not. And when Roy and their father got back from Vancouver and the disastrous bankruptcy swept all other considerations aside, their mother announced they'd be moving, once more, to a cheaper apartment across town. He never saw Chrissy Campbell again, but like most first experiences it was seared into his memory as with a branding iron.

VIII

In early May 1944, Lorne McRae found temporary work during the provincial election as an "organizer" for the Liberal party. Through the 1920s and '30s the Liberals had put together a formidable political machine and coasted on it comfortably with only one short Tory interruption. It was largely the creation of Premier Jimmy Gardiner, who had since moved on to Ottawa as federal Minister of Agriculture. The vaunted machine was used to dispense contracts and patronage, find civil service jobs for its preferred workers, stroke the Catholic Church which held sway with the immigrant farmers from central and eastern Europe, and get out the vote by strong canvassing and driving voters (often in government vehicles) to the polling stations. Gardiner had been Premier during the infamous Regina riot in July 1935 when the police charged and fired on a peaceful crowd of unemployed workers on a stopover in their protest trek to Ottawa, but he hoped that nine years later this ugly incident was mostly forgotten.

The Liberal machine had become old and arrogant and complacent. That it would hire a man like Lorne McRae as an organizer was probably a symptom of the party's senile decline. He didn't have much of a clue what he was doing, and spent most of his time trying to raise funds for the campaign without much success. Although the war had lifted the crushing burden of the depression, money was still hard to raise and most potential donors thought the Liberals had a shoo-in anyway.

They were wrong. On June 15, 1944, Saskatchewan elected the first avowedly socialist government in North America. Tommy Douglas became Premier of the new CCF (Cooperative Commonwealth

Federation) administration, and there was excitement in the air about changes expected in economic and social policy. Lorne McRae fulminated against the arrival of "the ignorant socialist hordes". The largest newspapers in the province, mainly the Regina *Leader-Post* and the Saskatoon *Star-Phoenix*, were owned by the same company, the Sifton Press, which was resolutely Liberal and led the chorus condemning the CCF as "regimenting state socialists". The CCF would nationalize the land and seize the people's farms, they trumpeted. Soviet-style communism was imminent. Some people, like Lorne McRae, took this seriously. So great was the fear-mongering and right wing rage spewed out in the local media that the CCF government investigated the cost of creating a new, friendly daily paper but decided it couldn't afford it. Largely unnoticed amid the hubbub in the press was the fact that Premier Douglas, already over-burdened with work, took on a double portfolio, also becoming Minister of Health.

The McRae household returned to some semblance of normalcy in July when Lorne found a job with the city as an assistant manager in the Municipal Transportation office, dispatching busses and streetcars and arranging for their maintenance and repair. Jean told her friends and neighbours that he was an "office manager". With the war still on there was a shortage of manpower and jobs were plentiful.

The boys hadn't seen much of Uncle Milt since the bankruptcy because Jean was too embarrassed to ask him over for meatloaf, but Milt invited himself to Sunday dinner saying that he'd bring along a roast if she'd cook it. I've missed home cooking lately, he said, and a prime rib must be done carefully to medium-rare even if the parsnips are well-done. Jean nodded assent and went ahead and cooked it to well done anyway, knowing that was the only way that Lorne would eat it. *Haute cuisine* had not yet found much of a foothold on the prairies. While the beef was being abused in the oven, Milt and the boys sat with a pitcher of lemonade at an old picnic table which the owner of the house had left in the back yard. Lorne continued to sit on the living room floor playing solitaire which was just fine with Milt.

The boys looked forward to a meal of roast beef and Milt said nothing about having brought the choice cut of meat and a store-bought lemon pie. Roy wanted to know if Milt could cook.

"Nope, never got the hang of it. Well, I generally make my own breakfasts and I am a dab hand at searing a steak, or I sometimes can manage stews or soups. Nothing fancy. Generally I eat pretty well in restaurants. Don't want to gain weight, you know. My girlfriends might not like it."

"It's nice that you have girlfriends, Uncle Milt," said Jamie, thinking of his own recent discovery of the pleasure of female company, "but how come you never got married?"

"I did, once, didn't you know? Oh, it was brief, and years ago. Once was enough. Now I'm not sure I want a woman around the house again, getting underfoot. Freedom has its compensations. I never seem to lack company."

"How long ago was your divorce?" Roy asked.

"Not divorced. My wife died, unexpectedly. It was years ago. I don't much talk about it. Time slides by. Let me think, how old are you, Jamie old son? Twelve, aren't you?"

"Thirteen."

"Right. I lose track. So I must have become a bachelor again the same year you were born, 1932. And Roy, you're eighteen I think? And ready for university?"

"Yes, Uncle Milt. Jamie skipped a grade, remember, and he'll be starting high school in September while I start university. That is, if I earn enough at my summer job in the bakery to pay the tuition. Then there's room and board and books and everything. Dad says he's not sure about it yet."

"I wouldn't worry about it. Maybe you'll take the first year at Regina College so you can save money by being at home. A bit of money can always be found for education, somewhere. I'll talk about it with your parents. Just assume you're going, okay? You'll love it. It's a great opportunity to learn and enjoy yourself and broaden your horizons. What do you want to be when you graduate?"

"Maybe a scientist, a physicist. I'm pretty sure I want to start in sciences and I'm interested in being a pilot. Flying would be really neat."

"I'll be a pilot, too," Jamie chimed in. "Whatever Roy does, I'd like to do. He has such great ideas, and I'll always go along with him. You bet. We're a team, aren't we Roy?"

"Damn right, we are. But you don't have to agree with me, or follow me if you don't want to. Every team needs different kinds of players, eh? I mean, we don't have to be the same, but we'll always … you know?"

"Roy's got that right, Jamie. You've got to be yourself."

"I guess so, but I'm not always as sure about things as he is. It just seems easier if Roy shows me what to do. Dad usually tells me, too, but I guess I depend more on Roy."

"Now, fellas, you've got the whole world ahead of you, your whole lives. When this war is over, I think in a year or two, you can do anything you like, be anything you choose. Do you know how wonderful it is to be starting out? Full of hopes and dreams. An old guy like me can only envy you. Say, have you been moving the coloured pins on your wall map of Europe to follow how bloody well our troops are doing? Damned if I don't think we're kicking a lot of Kraut arses since the invasion of Normandy in June. Great stuff, eh?"

So they talked a while about how the war was going and about how the world would be different and better when it was over. Milt thought it might take longer than most people believed to knock off the Japanese, fighting island to island. Then he looked at his watch and shouted in the door to ask Jean if dinner wasn't ready. She brought more lemonade and said no, not quite; the vegetables had taken more time and she'd been a bit slow getting everything into the oven. You boys have some more time yet.

Roy wanted to know Uncle Milt's opinions on the recent election. Could it be true, as the newspaper said, that the CCF would take away private property? Dad was convinced it was.

"No, of course not," Milt laughed. "If you believe that, I've got a bridge in Saskatoon that I'll sell you real cheap. They're just reformers with new ideas, some not so new at all. The federal Liberals have had public medical insurance in their platform since Mackenzie King became their leader in 1919. Promises, promises, and do you know what's happened? After twenty-five years? Nothing. Nothing at all. But I believe this Douglas fellow might be serious about it, if he can find the money. Saskatchewan is not what you'd call a rich province."

"Dad says he's a 'leftist'. Do you know what that means?" Jamie asked.

"Near as I can figure, it means a leftist wants to help ordinary people and the poor. Right wingers in politics tend to give the most help to business and the rich. It's not that simple, of course, but seems to me that's what it comes down to."

"I gather you trust this new guy," Roy said.

"I think so, at least so far. Already he's said that there'll be free medical and hospital services for cancer patients and for all old age pensioners *this year*, and hospital insurance for everyone by 1947. It will be grand when families faced with the costs of long term or terminal hospital care don't have to accept the grisly choice of selling the farm or calling the undertaker. Shows that his heart is in the right place, I'd say. Got a lot of good sense, for a Baptist."

"But you've also said, quite often, that you're not keen on priests and preachers," Roy observed, "that you're very skeptical about them and we should be, too."

"True enough, yeh, I've said that. But I guess that in politics, where there are no absolutes, the question is: compared to what? I gotta say that compared to this guy next door in Alberta, Premier Aberhart, Tommy sure looks good. Aberhart, hell, now there's a bible thumping asshole for you, pardon my French, droning on about Funny Money instead of actually doing something about education and health care and no-fault public automobile insurance and ...."

"Wait, Uncle Milt," Roy cut in, "what's 'funny money'?"

"Damned if I know. Mumbo-jumbo economics, is all I can say. Anyway, there's more I like about this little guy Douglas. Did you know he was Manitoba bantam-weight boxing champion when he was in college? Yup. I admire that. And apart from being a peppery little scrapper, I like that he quotes poetry so often in his speeches, apparently from memory, and also—I think this is important—he knows how to make people laugh. Doesn't take himself too seriously, as most damn preachers do. And he seems to have something to do with what they call 'the Social Gospel'."

"Never heard of it," said Roy.

"Long story short, it's a branch of the Protestants who are not much interested in all that bullroar about repressing the sins of the flesh or obsessed with getting in to heaven, much more interested in making a better world for mankind here below, trying to apply ethical teachings to social problems, trying to help people in their struggles with poverty and distress. 'Social justice' is their main theme, I guess, social salvation not just heavenly salvation, and helping people in real ways instead of praying at them."

"Sounds real good to me," Roy said.

"Me, too," Jamie agreed. "And you said laughter. Jokes? To make people feel good?"

"Sure, that, and to teach lessons about how to understand and how to cope. Let me give you an example of one of his stories, a sort of parable you might say. Here's how I remember it:

"Every four years in Mouseland, it being a democratic country, the mice held an election. Usually they'd elect the Black cats. Conditions for the mice were terrible, so soon they rose up in protest and voted out the Black cats and elected—White cats. The White cats preyed on the mice even more horribly than their predecessors, so next time, back in went the Black cats. Conditions got no better.

"Eventually a small mouse stood up in his corner and said, 'I think the trouble is that we elect cats, fat cats. So why don't we elect *mice?*' Other mice shook their heads and called him a radical, a communist. 'Lock him up,' they said, 'put him in jail.' But slowly the idea spread. Mice got the message. And the day came …."

Milt shook his head and smiled. "Tommy said the moral of the story is, you can lock up a mouse or a man, but you can't lock up an idea. Now, let's go inside and see about that roast before your mother burns it to a cinder."

IX

The McRae's fortunes changed. When the war ended in the summer of 1945 most people expected a return to depressed economic conditions, fearful that the troops returning home would have a tough time re-locating and finding jobs. Happily, even on the prairies, grim expectations can be wrong. Business boomed, particularly in the fields of housing and natural resources development, and in the public sectors of highway construction, hospital construction and rural electrification. Even Lorne McRae was soon able to find a better job, with Wallace Tractor and Equipment Ltd. as a salesman, mainly dealing in bulldozers and construction machinery. Jean's hopes of buying a house, a house with a garden and a fireplace, began to rise again. Lorne's ideas of investments, though, remained focused on penny stocks where he was confident that he'd strike it rich one day.

He talked a lot with his friend Aubrey Morrow, who had inherited some money, about the two of them going into business together, possibly starting a construction company. Lorne insisted that he could get great deals on bulldozers and road graders and gravel crushers, new or used, and that there was a lot of money to be made in highway construction. To prove his point he arranged to drive the skeptical Aubrey down to North Dakota and show him some new American road building techniques and some machinery that they could buy and import cheaply. The trip would take less than a week and was finally set for early October.

A difficulty arose when Jean told him he'd have to take the boys along. Lorne balked at this and told her not to be silly, it was a business trip and not a pleasure jaunt, but Jean was adamant that it would be "pleasant and educational", particularly for Jamie who had never travelled outside the province. It would mean only three days off school and Jamie was more than eager to go. Roy decided he couldn't, not wanting to miss hockey practices. Aubrey, whose own boys were grown up and away from home, said it was fine with him if Jamie rode quietly in the back seat of his 1941 Pontiac (new cars did not become available until the next year, 1946) and didn't talk too much. Lorne grumbled a lot, but agreed under pressure.

Jamie thought the trip was splendid. He read books as they rolled along over the prairie, some Robert Louis Stevenson and mostly Sinclair Lewis (including *Babbit*—he could relate to that small town promoter-salesman character without looking further than the front seat), and was alert also to the ways in which the U. S. seemed new and slightly different from home. He'd never thought the U. S. as "foreign" before, but he noticed that Americans seemed more open and friendly, less reserved than people he was used to, and that they enjoyed some roadside services not found back home. In particular he was interested in drive-ins for hamburgers and milkshakes and root beer, as well as what they called "motels", all of which appealed to him in the small cities they visited. In Minot and in Bismarck he saw his first drive-in movie theaters, and in Grand Forks, the place he liked best, after they'd checked in to a motel he thought was 'snazzy', Aubrey and his Dad had a couple of snorts of Wild Turkey bourbon while he sipped a coke, then drove in to the parking area surrounding a huge three-storey keg-like building with a neon sign proclaiming Hires' Root Beer. A girl attendant on roller skates took their order for hamburgers and soft drinks and, to his surprise, attached trays to the rolled down car windows.

"Isn't this swell, Dad? I sure like the way the diner is shaped like a barrel." (In his enthusiasm, he'd forgotten his father's antipathy to barrels.) "I'll bet a place like this in Regina would do a roaring business, don't you think?"

"I doubt it," said Lorne without turning around. "Too flashy. It probably won't last long here either and clearly will be shut down all winter. These Yankees get fancy new notions every now and again, then drop them just as quickly, wouldn't you say, Aubrey?"

"Sometimes, yes, but the boy might have a point. It might be a novelty worth considering. Could make a buck or two."

"Compared to the solid building of new highways, compared to real construction projects? I'd say bloody well not. Anyway, I thought you agreed, Jamie, not to talk a lot or interrupt serious business discussions." He waved a hand dismissively. "Now, about the Caterpillar war surplus dozers we'll look at tomorrow ...."

Jamie sighed and sat back in silence. He dowsed his thick burger with ketchup, stuck a straw into his root beer, and admired the bare legs of the waitresses in short shorts as they swirled on skates around the cars. He couldn't imagine that legs like those carrying trays of burgers and drinks would not be popular anywhere in the world. Later, looking back on it, he considered the Hires' Root Beer Keg one of the highlights of the trip.

When they returned to Saskatchewan their brief journey had some unexpected consequences. To the disappointment of Lorne, Aubrey decided not to be a player in the construction game and to invest in some apartment buildings and real estate instead. It seemed a lot simpler, and no engineers required. The more he thought about it the more bitter Lorne became. "Damned wasted trip, and not cheap, either."

Jamie told Roy all about it, about the motels and how he'd never seen one in Regina, and particularly how much he'd been impressed by the Keg drive-in diner. Roy said he could see how that would go over with the younger set, cruising around in their fathers' cars of an evening and no where to go except up and down Albert Street or out to the edge of the empty prairie and back. He promised Jamie he'd help him bring the subject up again with their Dad, although he doubted Lorne was likely to be receptive.

At dinner the next night Roy edged toward the diner idea and said he thought Jamie might be on to something; he'd seen drive-ins like that in movies.

"In movies, oh sure, you boys want me to start up something because you saw it in a movie. And I suppose you want me to sink a pile of money which I haven't got into some flash-in-the-pan Yankee foolishness, a fad that wouldn't last two years and of course couldn't operate in winter, and we'd sit watching it freeze up in a snow drift until spring when no one would remember what it was all in aid of anyway. If you think that makes any sense whatsoever you've got another think coming."

"Well, the motel thing could operate all year round," Roy persisted, "no matter what the weather, and people could plug in their cars' block heaters right at their doors. I sure do think it would work."

"And where do you young business geniuses think I'd raise the money to start up with? Selling apples? Robbing a bank?"

"Dad, think about it," Jamie urged. "You always say you know men with money to invest. You could borrow some or interest some friend in coming in as a partner and then you'd be your own boss, an owner. Maybe Uncle Milt would come in with us. But how much could it cost anyway, just for some asphalt paving and a couple of grills and an ice machine in a small building? Maybe an old Quonset hut from army surplus or even an old bus or a used-up streetcar trolley parked on blocks and made over. Wouldn't that work? You could even move a trolley like that to another location if you wanted."

Roy kept nodding encouragement but saw they weren't getting anywhere with their Dad who threw up his hands and began to growl at them impatiently.

"Oh sure, nothing to it. And your mother could become a short-order cook over a hot griddle. You think I want that? Do you? And after I hired workers, girls even, at the end of the season I'd just say, 'We're closing down, you're fired, g'bye.' Wouldn't that be a treat?"

Jamie had thought about it a lot and was nothing if not stubborn.

He looked at Roy for support and pressed on again.

"That's the beauty of it, don't you see? Roy is already in college, and I sure hope I soon will be, and we'll be wanting summer jobs. We could run the place. Minimum wage, probably, but I bet the tips would be real good. Summer jobs only, and we'd be able to hire our student friends and we could make it go, that's for darn sure."

"You two boys have answers for everything, don't you? Regular little Rockefellers. Everything except common sense and practical business experience and that little thing I mentioned, capital, ready money. Damned if I know why you keep ragging on it. Do me a favour and put a sock in it. I'm not interested. Burger joint, motel, bloody gold mines on the highway. In there any dessert, Jean?"

And so it was dropped, at least until Uncle Milt arrived for dinner two Sundays later. He was always indulgent of anything the boys had to say.

"I'm glad you liked your little trip, Jamie. Now what's this your mother tells me about some business idea or other? I'm amused at you trying to push your father into anything. Usually he's interested only in pie in the sky, but is this something about pie on the highway? Tell me about it."

Jamie was eager to tell. He blurted out his whole set of ideas with boyish enthusiasm and Roy backed him up, saying that it seemed to him Jamie was really using his head and might be on to something. It could be a big hit. More he thought about it, said Roy, maybe a motel would work right beside the drive-in to, what would you say, mutually reinforce each other and catch attention.

Milt smiled and rubbed his chin thoughtfully and asked a few questions, then smiled again and allowed that he'd stayed once in a motel in Billings, Montana, a year or so ago and liked it. The price was right and he'd found it convenient. No dragging of luggage up and down stairs. He said that in his opinion the food and drink business was always unpredictable, tricky, but just possibly there might be something to be said for a motel, more stable, particularly if he could find another angle, something extra. He rubbed his chin again and winked at Roy and slapped Jamie on the shoulder. That's using your noggin, Jamie me lad, that's good thinking, he beamed. Jamie always liked it when Uncle Milt called him 'Jamie me lad' or 'old sonny me boy'. It made him think that maybe he wasn't so dumb after all.

The upshot of it all was more than a year in unfolding. Milt, a cautious man but willing to entertain ideas from whatever source and however unlikely, did some thinking and made some inquiries about the Hotels Act and Liquor Control Act. It turned out that a motel could be legally a hotel under provincial legislation and that a motel could be licensed to sell alcohol and have a restaurant and also a beer parlour. Milt regarded a beer hall as a licence to print money. Quietly he put together a group of two other investors and incorporated the Bluebird Motor Inn and Lounge. Although he put a couple of shares each in the names of Jamie and Roy McRae he did not mention this to anyone in the family. Let's just see how this plays out, he thought.

It was months later, in the spring, when Lorne drove by a construction site on the edge of town and noticed a sign for the Bluebird. He stopped the car. "Inn and Lounge" the sign read, unmistakably. That could only mean one thing. Damn it all to hell. Why, oh for Christ's sake, why hadn't he thought of that?

At dinner Roy was out playing basketball but Lorne confronted and upbraided Jamie.

"About that notion you had for a motel last year. Why in the name of God didn't you tell me that a motel was a hotel?"

"I guess I didn't think to call it that. But it seemed obvious. Why?"

"You didn't think of that? You didn't tell me that a motel could be licensed like a hotel and serve alcohol? And have a beer parlour? You didn't bloody well think of that?"

"Does it matter, Dad? I mean, a motel is just a different kind of hotel. I don't much see that it matters. You didn't seem all that interested, whatever Roy and I said. I mean, I'm not sure I see the problem. Why are you getting mad about what it's called?" He looked at his mother for help, but she stared at her plate.

"You don't see the problem! You don't see the flaming problem! You nagged and yammered on about a motel and even that crap about a drive-in diner, and in all that blather you didn't say the most important thing, that your bloody motel could have a bar and a beer parlour and be a goldmine, an absolute money machine and a goldmine."

"That part of it never occurred to me, or to Roy. Should it have? We were just trying to tell you, to persuade you …. I mean, we were just trying to be helpful."

But Lorne continued to shout and bang things. He roared "I suppose I've got to think of everything around here" and "damned know-it-all kids with no common sense". Then he got his coat and slammed out of the house.

"What in the world was that all about, Mom?"

"Oh, your father seems to think he missed out on something, dear, that's all. When people make big mistakes, you'll find, they usually try to put the blame on someone else, not on themselves. It's human nature, I expect, nothing you can change and nothing you should worry about. Now, do finish your pork chop, there's a good boy, and I'll see what I can find for dessert."

Jamie didn't feel much like eating.

One other development which may or may not have been an indirect result of the trip to North Dakota took a longer time to unfold. Roy had told some of his buddies at school about how clever he thought his brother's idea was for a drive-in diner. Two of his friends, Gerry and Gabe, liked the sound of that and talked about it to Gerry's dad who owned a restaurant downtown on Rose Street where the two boys often filled in on weekends as grill men or working the front counter. They were quick to see the appeal of the idea.

By the following spring Gerry and Gabe opened the G & G drive-in burger and shake joint at the end of Albert Street south, using a defunct trolley car as their base. It was immediately popular and started coining money. They expanded the next year to a second location east of the city on Highway #1 and were even more successful.

Jamie and Roy took a certain wry satisfaction in the way the drive-ins were such a big hit and flourished, although they knew enough not to talk about that in front of their testy father. With Uncle Milt it was another story. He laughed about it a lot and often took the boys to the G & G Albert Street diner in the evening or on a Sunday afternoon. Their mother sometimes came along; their father never did.

Milt laughed even harder when, several years later, he heard the story of how Gerry and Gabe had been visited at their east side location by an odd looking man in a white suit with a string tie and a pointy Van Dyke beard. He said he was from Kentucky. People called him the Colonel. Name of Sanders. Would the boys be interested in a franchise deal he had on offer involving southern fried chicken? Maybe, said Gerry. I guess so, said Gabe, why not? Soon they were spending their winters in 'Vegas or Florida as the money rolled in.

Milt just loved that story. "Funny old thing, this life," he often said, "when fate sneaks up behind you and offers either a kick in the arse or a blessing on your head. Sometimes, though, it's not clear which is which until you decide for yourself how to react. There are times when an apparent blessing makes you complacent, and times when a swift kick in the keester can wake you up to pay attention and to try harder. It's very hard to say."

Long before anyone ever heard of Colonel Sanders, however, when Gerry and Gabe had just opened their first drive-in, Jamie and Roy were enjoying G & G burgers and shakes with Milt in his brand new 1947 Chrysler and they couldn't help complaining how closed and resistant their father had been to any suggestions about novelties in curb-side food or motels. He's a real stick-in-the-mud, Roy lamented.

"Now hold on, fellas," Milt said, "you must always show respect for a father who tries. He's basically a good man and he's always worked hard and looked out for you two. Maybe he's a bit set in his ways, not quick to recognize new methods of doing things, but most people aren't either, and he's never had the advantages, like some, of a fistful of money in a savings account to take business risks with. It's damned hard to be short of money and that can weigh you down and cramp your mind. A run of disappointments can form a helluva black cloud to live under, make a person sour. It's not always a man's fault if he's behind the eight ball, usually it's just bad luck, and God knows life isn't fair. So I don't want to hear you saying anything against your dad. Every father deserves respect, you hear me?"

Both boys nodded, although Jamie remained less than convinced. It crossed his mind that Uncle Milt might be feeling guilty about having so many disagreements with their father, or maybe about having more money, or maybe he was getting soft.

"Anyway," Milt added, "there's an old saying that the best time to make a really sweet investment is always 'last year'."

"Have you always had it pretty easy?" Roy wondered.

"Me? Nope, not really. Had to hustle and work my butt through college to get the law degree, and then had some lean years. Got conned into borrowing once for a bad investment in a mining company and when it didn't pan out the main owner disappeared with almost all of the assets, just like one of your dad's experiences. Had my share of good luck and bad luck, like most people. Say, I've never told you about a run-in I had with a couple of thugs on the road once? Oh yeh, they tried to rob me, and I had a satchel of cash on the seat of the car beside me that I was taking to a man for a real estate transaction.

"It was just northwest of here, near those Asian market gardens. I got a flat tire on my old Ford and climbed out to change it. Two guys appeared from out of the field, rough looking fellows, but I didn't pay full attention because I thought they were coming to help me. I smiled and started to wave them off, saying I was okay with it, when the bigger one grabbed me around the neck in a choke hold from behind and the smaller one waved a knife and demanded my wallet and car keys. Couldn't go along with that, now could I? Luckily I still had the tire iron in my hand. I swung back at the big guy, low and hard, and broke his knee. The one with the knife was so startled that he hesitated and I was able to lay the iron on him too and I think I broke his wrist. The two of them made off back into the field as fast as their three legs could carry them."

"Did you call the police? Did they get caught?"

"Nah, I thought they'd learned a lesson and anyway, whatthehell, no witnesses and my one word against their two in a court case that would waste time. Nope, what I did was sit down on the car's running board and laugh. With relief, you know. And then I broke into a cold sweat and thought what a damn close call it had been, and then I laughed some more and drove away. Never much liked market gardens again, though." And he laughed some more.

"Anyhow," he continued, "never doubt, lads, that you can do anything you have to do, and don't take shit from anybody. But I'd be glad if you didn't repeat that story to your parents or anyone else. I've never told it before, except to my late wife, of course. Don't want people to think that I'm a roughneck, do we?" And he laughed again.

The boys looked at him with even deeper admiration and respect than usual. Quite the guy, Uncle Milt.

X

The thing Jamie liked best about high school was that he made new friends. His mother extracted a promise from the father that, even if they had to move again, they would not leave the area of Central Collegiate so that Jamie would not have to change schools. This proved not to be an issue because sales of bulldozers continued briskly and Lorne made a pretty good income. Not a large income, but one that Jean could say was "respectable", although she never knew how much it was and her "household allowance" didn't increase by much. To the boys their mother seemed to be slower, aging, more pale and less chirpy. Jean sometimes supplemented her income by doing a little work for cousin Milt in his office in the McCallam-Hill building, mostly bookkeeping—on his current accounts only, never his savings or capital account—but there wasn't much to do most months because Milt always had a secretary-typist who kept the office in good order. He kept careful track of Jean's hours because he thought his cousin was looking tired, strained.

Friends became more important to Jamie when Roy entered second year university in Saskatoon. He didn't come home much, it seemed to Jamie not often enough. Classes and lab work kept him very busy, Roy wrote, and he worked part time as a waiter in the Barootes family's restaurant on Second Avenue, the Patricia, to keep himself financially afloat. In notes and postcards home and the occasional letter he reported that he was getting very good grades, but sometimes he felt rather tired, as though he was overdoing it a bit. He still played hockey with the varsity Huskies although he thought he might have lost a bit of pep.

Nothing to fuss about, of course, and the university Health Service had good doctors who looked after students very well.

Jamie asked if he could go up to Saskatoon to visit his brother, maybe by train or bus, but his father said he couldn't afford that at the moment. He could hitch-hike, Jamie persisted, but Jean said no son of hers would thumb rides like a bum and that was that.

One of the things he wanted to talk with Roy about was erections. He kept having them at unexpected and distinctly inconvenient times. Not just at the movies, as when he watched Rita Hayworth begin a tantalizing strip tease in *Gilda* and had to wait ten minutes after the movie ended until he could walk out of the theatre without a bulge in his pants, but also on the street or in school. Girls' round bottoms really got to him, and often he got a stiff reaction to the backs of knees in nylons above snow boots.

Roy had warned him he had to be "careful with, you know, emissions" because of their mother. When she'd noticed evidence of a wet dream on his bed sheets, she'd demanded that their father speak to Roy about "the problem", but Dad didn't want to know about it and got surly and remained silent. Mother glared at Roy and wouldn't talk to him for two days. Finally she said she was "deeply disappointed" in him, and muttered "dirty" several times, "dirty". So Roy had got the message, and recommended great caution to his brother.

This only perplexed and distressed Jamie more. In fact, without Roy's guidance, he found the whole subject of sex confusing. Weren't love and sex the same thing, and wasn't love good? Or were they different and separate? Could you have sexual feelings without love, or were you supposed to be in love without feeling horny urges? It was a puzzlement. His persistent erections disturbed and embarrassed him. Could it be that he was abnormal, maybe some kind of pervert?

And then there was the problem of his hot crush on his French teacher, Jeannie Shaw. He didn't like French and hated verb charts, but Miss Shaw's fiery Irish red hair and bright blue eyes fascinated him, reminding him of Chrissy Campbell. He found it hard to pay much attention to what she said, yet loved the lyrical way she said it. Although Miss Shaw was painfully thin, a young stick-lady without much figure, her long slender legs were nice and she had tremendous energy. He couldn't take all that "plume de ma tante" stuff seriously, but he couldn't stop staring at her intensely when she was in the room. "Just a bad case of puppy love," one of his classmates assured him, even though that didn't much help him to contain his feelings. It's difficult to learn French if you're sitting in a classroom with a textbook perched over a frequent and bothersome erection.

During one afternoon class after a routine fire drill Miss Shaw lit into the group for talking and shouting in the hall and returning too slowly to their seats. She went into a tirade about "sloppy and disorderly conduct." Her eyes blazed around the room and lit on Jamie. "And wipe that smirk off your face this second!" He raised a quizzical index finger to his chest and blinked. "Yes, you. I don't care what your marks are, just get rid of that smirk, now!" He did. Soon she calmed down and resumed the conjugation of the verb être.

After the class, dismayed that he had given offense, Jamie approached her desk and began to mumble an apology. She fixed him with a level gaze. "And just why, may I ask, were you grinning?" "I didn't realize I was grinning, really, Miss Shaw. It was just that I couldn't help smiling at how pretty you look when you're angry. I'm sorry if that was wrong." She stared at him uncertainly. "Oh. I see. Well, you may go, Jamie. And thank you for — your apology. That will be all." He marched away, unsure of whether he'd fallen deeper into her bad books, or not. At least he hadn't had an erection.

Another of his favourite teachers, Vera Creighton, an old dear who taught history, liked one of Jamie's oral presentations in class and suggested that he might be interested in the Public Speaking and Debating Club. He didn't know anything about it except that it had been organized that year by Richard (Dick) Slater, a grade ten student who was president of his tenth grade form, and since Jamie was president of his grade nine form, the two of them had nodded at each other at Students' Council meetings. It soon proved that they had several interests in common including movies, chess, CBC radio, and particularly politics and oratory since they'd both heard Premier T. C. Douglas often on the radio. Jamie quickly came to regard this as the basis for a solid friendship for life.

Unlike his own father, Dick's dad was a supporter of the CCF. An M. A. in psychology, Ted Slater was a senior official in the provincial Department of Education, now in charge of planning and implementing what were called Larger School Districts which were gradually replacing the traditional one-room rural schoolhouses. When they met, Jamie was tremendously impressed by Mr. Slater who was, apart from two or three high school teachers, the first "intellectual" he'd ever encountered.

As it turned out, Dick and Jamie had a mutual friendship with another member of the Students' Council, Helen Rivkin, also in grade ten, another strand in the cat's cradle which linked them. Helen's parents too were brainy people, recently arrived from New York, the Bronx, because they wanted to be part of what they'd heard was a "socialist experiment" in Saskatchewan. The mother, Rose, was a painter and the father, Abe, was a doctor and a specialist in public health who worked for the Department of Health. Helen often asked Dick and Jamie (whom she always called 'Red') whether they'd seen the latest contributions of Benchley or Dorothy Parker or Heywood Broun in *The New Yorker.* They hadn't even heard of that magazine, but both began to go to the school library to read it faithfully, and not merely for the cartoons which neither of them initially would admit that they didn't always understand. Was a seal in a bedroom really funny? Could be, but …. Jamie's favourites became Dorothy Parker for the biting wit of her poems and an essayist named Alexander Woolcott who wrote in a slightly arch and archaic if not quaint style. His essay "Colossal Bronze" on the great negro actor and singer Paul Robeson gave Jamie one of his first life-long heroes and an addiction to *The New Yorker* that never ceased to open new doors.

His other idols at the time were Babe Ruth and Franklin D. Roosevelt. It seemed natural that heroes had to be huge commanding figures doing great things in important distant places. It had not yet occurred to him that his principal hero through all the years would prove to be a short unassuming preacher in his own home province.

It was clear to Jamie that Helen and her parents came from another world. They had an expensive record player and a collection of disks that ranged from Beethoven to Verdi and Duke Ellington to an earthy folk singer named Woody Guthrie. They read books that they owned and did not come from the public library. On their walls hung paintings done by Rose, some of which were called "abstracts", and prints by Van Gogh and Modigliani, including (gulp) a reclining nude. They laughed and joked a lot and ate strange food they called "deli", unheard of things such as smoked meat and knishes and latkes and blintzes. Jamie considered the Rivkins to be the most exotic and sophisticated beings in the world, and even Dick was impressed.

The three of them made an unlikely trio. Helen was short and chubby with black curly hair and blinked a lot behind thick glasses. Her dark eyes were merry and her wide face expressive. She had a loud voice and a throaty laugh like Tallulah Bankhead. Jamie's red hair and pale white skin provided him with a sunburned nose every summer and acne in the winter which embarrassed him. He was tall and thin, but not as lean as Dick who was very bony with a coal black pompadour, thin lips, a chiseled face with a prominent nose, and alert gray eyes that darted and probed. Helen often suggested that the three of them go to movies together, and they saw things like Olivier's *Hamlet* and *The Red Shoes*, and *Oliver Twist* and *The Third Man*.

But it was Dick Slater and the Public Speaking and Debating Club that occupied most of Jamie's time and attention. Being a grade behind and almost two years younger at an age when such differences seemed vast, he often had to cope with Dick's popularity and immense number of older friends when the two of them walked down the street together. People were always attracted to Dick and wanted him to stop and talk. He was "a character" even then, off-beat and interesting and funny. As well as being a "slap 'em up, chuff 'em up Charlie" sort of guy with an ebullient personality, perhaps preparing himself even in grade ten for a run at the presidency of the Students' Council and for later political campaigning, Jamie sensed in him an inner core of reserve and sturdy self-reliance, just as Roy had, although it wasn't part of Dick's public presentation. That stiff backbone and quick mind came out mostly when the two of them were alone and often arguing. They loved to argue.

With help from speakers' handbooks and from their best and favourite English teacher, Jed Howard, they learned to structure formal debates in the Club, to do research on a topic and to make their prepared speeches clear and logical, presenting their cases with vigor if not intellectual depth. Preparation was a serious learning experience. They were so earnest about it that a drama coach was brought in by the school from the YWCA to give them several lessons in voice and speech. Within two years Dick and Jamie had won every local and regional trophy in high school debating. In Dick's senior year they enlisted Bill Whitefield, said to have the highest IQ ever recorded in Central Collegiate, to help them as a three-man team to challenge first year university students at nearby Campion and Luther Colleges, debating issues like, Resolved: That the Canadian Senate should be Abolished; That Canada should Join the United States; That the CBC should be Privatized; That the British should Abandon India. They seldom lost a contest.

But what Jamie and Dick liked best was to argue with each other for the sheer hell of it. It was their favourite form of conversation. They argued at school after class and after Students' Council meetings, in each other's homes, in Scotty's Grill across from the school, after movies, or just walking down the street. They argued about Rome *vs.* Greece after writing history essays, about Kipling *vs.* Hemingway, whether the

Liberal government of Canada was reactionary, whether Rita Hayworth was more beautiful than Gene Tierney, whether the Saskatchewan Roughriders were better than the Calgary Stampeders, whether the sun would rise in the east next morning. Oddly enough it did not seem to matter which side the other took; they would often switch sides and re-hash their arguments in new forms the next day. It was mainly a matter of mental gymnastics and verbal sparring, not a matter of declaring a winner, as though each needed the other to practice and validate their cuts and thrusts.

It often amused them that some other friend would say how sorry he was that they'd had such a loud shouting match and falling out. They'd both laugh at that. The main thing about their verbal jousting is that they both enjoyed it. They got along like cakes and ale. Their running contest made them close, best friends. Rivalry can be as bonding as ribaldry.

And there was lots of ribaldry too when they talked about girls they were going to ask to the next dance or brag about sexual conquests they'd made, well, almost, and were certain they'd make next weekend, with their triumphs evasively phrased in what the grammar text called "the future conditional" tense.

Still, Jamie spent most of his high school years dreamily in the throes of love. Once with a delicious little blonde whose family then moved away, out of town and out of reach, next with a fleeting series of short term hopeful crushes, then with a dazzling brunette with merry eyes named Lorraine who tantalized and rewarded him with unbuttoned blouses and exciting stocking tops, black garters over creamy white thighs, but denied him the Promised Land.

At the regular sock hops in the school gym he spent a lot of time leaning on a wall and admiring girls wistfully as they jived to records like Count Basie's 'One O'clock Jump' or Charlie Barnett's 'Redskin Rumba'. For most of one year his idea of heaven was to slow-dance with Carol Wright to Hoagy Carmichael's musical ache, 'Stardust', played by

Tommy Dorsey. But Carol was just a friend, the social director on the students' council, one grade ahead of him with a steady boyfriend away at university, who used him only as a convenient date, avoiding any close encounters of the sweaty kind.

Dick and Jamie agreed that the important thing was both of them getting to university and both studying law so that they could form a partnership as McRae and Slater, or more likely Slater and McRae, Barristers and Solicitors. It was understood that Jamie would do the legal research and draft the briefs and that Dick would perform eloquent miracles of prodigious persuasion in the courtroom. Probably Dick would run for political office and Jamie would run the law firm.

What they were not sure of was a political affiliation. Both took politics very seriously and both were enthusiastic admirers of the new Premier, Tommy Douglas. Jamie was a devoted believer in what Tommy said, while Dick was more cynical about whether the CCF would come a cropper, lacking staying power, and was mostly a fan not so much of what Tommy said but how he said it. The style seemed to appeal more to Dick than the substance.

At least some of this difference was apparently resolved when the two of them were able to spend a couple of days alone at the Slater's family cottage in the Qu'Appelle Valley at B-Say-Tah beach alone over an Easter weekend. With snow still on the ground and a bootlegged case of twenty-four beer, plus a satchel of canned meat and wieners and beans, they settled down for two days to continue their interminable arguments. Dick had brought from his father's library two Pelican books on British politics, *A Case for Socialism* by Fred Henderson and Quentin Hogg's *A Case for Conservatism*. On the first night each read one of these short books and then presented the leading arguments. The next day they replenished their supplies with twelve more beer, traded off and read the other book, and settled down to a long night's wrangle over which political case was the more convincing. By dawn they were exhausted and bleary. The sun rose on a still skeptical Dick Slater who never wanted to see or smell fried Spam again but allowed as how he might join a CCF youth group, and Jamie McRae who had decided he was definitely a socialist.

What is it that causes young people to embrace a political position? Many people vote the way their families have always voted and don't give it a thought. Canadian Catholics strongly incline toward the Liberal party, Anglicans toward the Tories. Wealthy people were mainly right wingers for whichever old-line party seemed most pro-business at the time; poor people and workers were more likely to be interested in the left. Some people couldn't care less either way and seldom voted. Others seemed to need an ideology as a sort of religion to give them a sense of purpose and belonging. And then there were those like Jamie, who were ready to take almost any political stance that was in contradiction to their father's, a sort of *épater les pères* as a sign of rebellion. His dad liked machinery, Jamie liked books; the father loved horseradish, the son hated it. But Jamie had become a whole-hearted convert. Mrs. McRae was not at all surprised when her son shunned the Liberals and declared himself a democratic socialist. Family tensions often play out in different ways in public, although guardedly, without making home life any smoother.

Henderson's *Case* was very strong and simple. Greed was not a grand basis for a moral economy. Monopolies did not react to the market but rigged the market, and should be regulated – or publically owned. Distribution of income favoured owners and the powerful and deprived the poor, particularly the unemployed, of life's essentials. A just society would address and adjust the extremes of inequality so that ordinary people could have increased access to higher education, health services, and income security during infirmity and old age. And the desire for reduced inequality was a moral demand, consistent with the ethical teachings of all great religions, including the Commandment of Jesus that you shall love your neighbour as yourself. An unfair world could be made more fair.

It was this last fundamental principle which resonated most in Jamie. It seemed to him obvious and compelling, and it quickened his interest in their own socialist Premier.

When the two boys heard that Tommy Douglas was to address a Hi-Y youth convention of the YMCA, of which they were not members, they were determined to hear him. Dick's father knew the director of the Regina Y and arranged for them to get in. Jamie found Mr. Douglas fascinating and was swept along by the wit and magnetism of the man. Short in stature, his presence still seemed to dominate and illuminate the room. Tommy's glasses glinted and his smile gleamed as he spoke of the duty to work for social improvement and one's fellow man, with party or politics never mentioned. He quoted Robbie Burns as he loved to do:

> The rank is but the guinea's stamp,
> The man's the gold, for a' that.

This was followed by the old chestnut, "Abou Ben Adhem" by Leigh Hunt.

> Abou Ben Adhem, may his tribe increase,
> Awoke one night from a deep dream of peace
> And saw, within the moonlight in his room,
> Making it rich, like a lily in bloom,
> An Angel writing in a Book of Gold.
>
> Exceeding peace made Ben Adhem bold,
> And to the presence in the room he said,
> "What writest thou?" The vision raised its head
> And with a look made of all sweet accord, answered,
> "The names of those who love the Lord."
>
> "And is mine one?" said Abou.

"Nay, not so," replied the Angel.
Abou spoke more low but cheerly still
And said, "Pray then, write me as one
Who loves his fellow man."
The Angel wrote and vanished.

The next night, the Angel came again
In a great awakening light
To read the names of those whose love the Lord had blessed,
And lo, Ben Adhem's name led all the rest!

That poem made Jamie feel much better about being a pagan, not out of place and re-assured in his beliefs, although Dick found it a bit banal.

The *pièce de resistance* was no less a boys' school cliché, Kipling's "If", but Tommy's reading (or presentation from memory) made it seem real and immediate, as though the Premier was speaking to Jamie personally:

If you can keep your head when all about you
Are losing theirs and blaming it on you,
(Did you know that, Dad? Do you know that?)
If you can meet with Triumph and Disaster
And treat those two impostors just the same;

★   ★   ★   ★   ★

If you can fill the unforgiving minute
With sixty seconds worth of distance run,
Yours is the Earth and everything that's in it,
And—which is more—you'll be a Man, my son!

Of such moments hero worship is created.

Jamie later told his mother and Uncle Milt that he'd never felt so moved or so inside of a poem until Tommy's perfect diction and heartfelt sincerity made the words come alive for him as never before. So much so that at the end of the speech he gathered up his courage to go down to the front of the room and stand in line to shake the Premier's hand.

Up close, Tommy was a slight man of perhaps one hundred and forty or fifty pounds, quick and erect, with small features, a laughing mouth, and light brown hair curling up into an obstinate lock above a high forehead. Although Jamie stood almost six feet tall and the Premier only five foot six, he felt he was looking up at Tommy, a powerful elevated presence encased in energy and magnetism. "Oh, yes," said Mr. Douglas, "I know you. My daughter Shirley goes to your school and she tells me that you and your friend Dick Slater are the coming young debaters. Good for you. Let me know if there's ever anything I can do for you." Jamie blinked and mumbled his thanks and withdrew, feeling as though he'd just been recognized by royalty. He never forgot the encounter.

Only a few weeks after that event Jamie and Dick snuck out of school in the afternoon to hear Mr. Douglas again. Dick's father had told them that Tommy was going to deliver a major speech in the legislature on the subject of war and peace. It was February and the ice was frozen so they cut across Wascana Lake to the House and found seats in the gallery facing the government bench.

The Premier's address pleased them extravagantly.

> One has only to look at the world around us and see totalitarian communism on one hand and monopoly-ridden capitalism on the other to realize that social democracy offers mankind its best hope of survival .... Over the world scene hangs the greatest fear of all — the fear of nuclear war and the possible annihilation of mankind ....
>
> [Another] danger to which we are exposed is that of absorption, culturally and economically by the United States. We are not anti-American. We do not dislike Americans though we abhor American

imperialism in all its manifestations. But then, so do many Americans ....

Mr. Speaker, ... giving people security, giving people good health, giving people the feeling of well-being, is the most important defence there is against Communism. Communities where people have security and where care is taken of the needy and unfortunate have the kind of society into which Communism has never been able to infiltrate ....

I hear people talking about defending democracy. You may have to defend it with bayonets and bombs, but in the final analysis democracy is an idea which cannot be defended with guns and bombs alone. The greatest way to defend democracy is to make it work ....

The next day when the boys faced the school's vice principal, Mr. Clarke, for playing hookey, he laughed and said, "Now you know that Saskatchewan is the only province with a foreign policy. And I think I'll send your names in to the Guinness Book of Records as the only students who ever played truant to listen to a politician. Tell you what; I'll decrease your detentions to only two hours. The truth is, I'm sort of partial to Mr. Douglas myself."

XI

It was not exactly clear how or why Roy disappeared. There was an element of casualness about it as though he might re-appear next week or next month or at any time.

He had mailed a short letter to the family which seemed enigmatic at best, certainly vague.

My Dear Parents,

I have something awkward to tell you.

Some problems have come up that I'm not just sure how best to deal with. After a lot of thought I've decided to drop out of school and take some time off, probably an extended time, so I won't be in touch for a while. I may go traveling. Please don't worry about me. It would take me much too long to explain everything and I wouldn't want you to fret about how I'm feeling, but I'm sure I'm doing the right thing. I'll just get out of the way for a time. One day I'm sure you'll understand. This seems to me the way to cause the least trouble.

All my love,

Roy

P.S. Please tell Jamie not to worry either. He's a great little brother— well, not so little any more— and there's never been a day go by that I haven't thought of him with love and pride.

R.

This letter startled the McRaes, but left them more confused than frightened. They felt confident of Roy's fundamental good sense and that he'd turn up soon, although they couldn't begin to imagine what had happened. Would he lose is university year? Had he become depressed about some unexpected setback? Maybe he'd fallen in love and followed a girl off on some trip. His mother's mind raced and skittered across hundreds of unlikely possibilities, and Lorne found himself trying to visualize innumerable scenarios, some as far-fetched as seeing his son in the Foreign Legion as "Beau Geste", but nothing he could dream up made much sense to him. For now, all they could do was wait. And hope.

Altnough Lorne kept telling her to try to relax and wait for news, her mother's instinct made Jean sure that something dire and extreme had happened. Her days of stabbing anxiety and growing fear stetched into a week, and more. Her ordeal of convulsive nightmares often left her choking and gasping in anguish. Every day she phoned the police about a missing person and the various hospitals about new admissions. She resorted to abject pleading in her prayers. Her despair turned her to seek guideance from "psychics" and grinning fortune tellers. She found it difficult to eat or to read or to concentrate on anything that did not pertain to her son. She succumbed to quivering emotional distres that left her weak and exhausted, hollwed.

And still there was no word from Roy.

Jamie had found his brother's letter stunning and utterly baffling. Why hadn't Roy written to him, or 'phoned? He regarded Roy as totally competent, able to deal with absolutely anything, so what might have thrown him off the rails was beyond his comprehension. Surely Roy knew that he would do anything for him, walk over hot coals for him if he'd ask. Why hadn't he asked? Why had he not come home to talk about it?

"Tell Jamie not to worry." What in hell was that supposed to mean? Roy knew damn well he'd worry, in fact couldn't sleep for dark forebodings.

One cold and sunless morning Jamie rose early, threw some bread and cheese and a jar of peanut butter into his schoolbag, left a note for his parents to say where he was going, and set off for Saskatoon to see whether he could find Roy. He travelled by thumb, hitchhiking, and luckily caught a ride with a shoe salesman as far as Davidson, the halfway point. From there he found another lift on to Saskatoon, where he'd never been before, and was pleasantly surprised that the entire trip took him only four hours.

A bus took him over the 25th Street bridge to the university where he quickly found the men's residence, Qu'Appelle Hall, and, shortly afterwards, Roy's roommate, John Fillipiuk, whom everyone called Johnny Flip.

No, Flip didn't understand it either. No, Roy had said nothing about leaving, hadn't left a note, or been in touch since. It's just that when Flip got up late one morning, his friend was not there. Hadn't seen hide nor hair of him since. No, he hadn't talked about any particular problem. Depressed? Well, he hadn't seemed his usual happy self; not depressed, maybe a bit down, more quiet. Pre-occupied, sort of. But he'd missed few if any classes, seemed to be studying, had been to hockey practice the previous day, he was pretty sure.

Anyway, Flip said he'd told all that to the Dean of Residence and to the Registrar, and to the police when they got a missing person report from the university, as well as to the man who showed up yesterday, an uncle. Milt? Yup, that was the man, Mr. Milton. He'd shown Flip his lawyer's card and some ID, also a photo from his wallet of Roy and Jamie and himself. After they'd talked a while, Flip had found Roy's old trunk and helped Milt pack up his things, not a lot of stuff, books and notes and photos mostly, and gave him a hand carrying it down to the car. Left most of Roy's clothes in the closet, in case he showed up. Offered to buy me lunch, which was nice of him, seemed a real good guy, but I had to beg off because of a one o'clock class. Said he'd be driving back to Regina that night, quite late. And he told me that I was welcome to use any of Roy's stuff that I wanted, because he seemed to feel that Roy probably wouldn't be back before the end of term.

That afternoon, still disconsolate, Jamie took a walk through the campus but didn't much feel like going downtown to look around town like a tourist. His head swimming in fears and doubts, he walked down to the river and sat by the water, gnawed at by thoughts and memories, feeling incomplete. He hadn't really found out anything useful. Toward the end of the day he realized he'd missed lunch and was hungry. A slow walk back to Roy's room put him again in the company of Johnny Flip who lent him a dollar to buy a hamburger at Bell's Drugstore across the road and said he could spend the night in the room, in Roy's bed. He felt vaguely uncomfortable sleeping there but had little choice, and passed a restless dream-filled night.

At dawn he rose and made his way back to the highway to hitch a ride south with a farmer in a pick-up truck who talked endlessly about the Wheat Pool and grain prices, but he didn't listen.

At home Sunday evening Uncle Milt was there for dinner. With his parents he and Milt went over and over their stories of what questions they'd asked, how very little they'd found out, what conjectures and speculations were on their minds. Soon the dinner lapsed into a strained silence. After they'd toyed with dessert Milt and Jamie went out to sit on the front steps but still couldn't find much more to say.

Finally Jamie said, "I wish you'd told me you were driving up to Saskatoon. I'd have liked to go with you."

"Yes, I'm sorry about that. I guess I was too upset to be thinking straight. Just jumped into the car and headed north fast. My mind was totally on Roy. I didn't think about anybody else, even you, until I was many miles up the road, right past Craik. I certainly am sorry. I just goofed, Jamie-me-lad. I apologize."

"Sure. Okay. And I was wondering, why did you tell Flip not to expect Roy back before the end of term? Any reason?"

"What? Did I say that? Well, no reason. Just a feeling, Jamie. Just a feeling. One I'd be more than happy to be wrong about, that's for damn sure."

They lapsed into silence again and soon called it a night, each trapped in his own dark thoughts.

XII

When Dick Slater and Helen Rivkin went up to the University of Saskatchewan in 1950, Jamie McRae followed them to Saskatoon the next year, re-uniting their high school trio. They all found the university atmosphere free and stimulating. Dick majored in history, liking British and French history best, particularly the lives of Disraeli and Napoleon. Helen did English lit. with a minor in drama. It was economics and political science that attracted Jamie who considered them useful background for the study of law. He also sat in on, or "audited", some literature courses, American poetry and drama with Carlyle King and the English novel with Doug Cherry, although the Department of Political Economy discouraged his dabbling in lit. as "unprofessional" if he wanted to be a serious economist. Until then it had never occurred to him that university administrators would want to restrict the range of his intellectual curiosity. It was an early and salutary lesson in the rigidities of institutional bureaucracies.

His mind was always set on studying law because of his commitment to Dick that they would form a partnership in a legal firm that was sure to flourish based on their friendship, their complementary skills, and Dick's high visibility in debating and student politics. He was an extremely popular guy and getting set for a run at student council president.

In preparation for law, apart from pursuing the B.A., they both read widely about lawyers, from Irving Stone's *Clarence Darrow for the Defense* to works by and about Oliver Wendell Holmes. Occasionally they'd trot down to the court house in Saskatoon to listen to trial work by distinguished counsel like Emmett Hall and 'Bud' Estes and John Diefenbaker, all of which made legal studies more real and immediate to them, certain as they were that they would be litigators.

With their pal Helen they continued to chortle over Tommy Douglas stories. The leader of the Liberal opposition was a ponderous, huge and fat lawyer named Walter Tucker. They laughed a lot, as many people did, at the Liberal campaign slogan of "Tucker or Tyranny" as the opposition and the anti-CCF daily papers continued to accuse the government of being communist. They government quietly went ahead with the programs to protect farmers from foreclosure by mortgage companies in years of crop failures, extension of sewer and water services to small towns and villages, rural electrification, public ownership of a province-wide bus service, no-fault public automobile insurance, and an air ambulance system. Douglas was so popular that people repeated the line: "Tommy doesn't kiss babies. Babies kiss him."

Jamie particularly liked a Douglas thrust from a debate with Tucker at Crystal Falls, near Yorkton. Tucker said he'd been in favour of the national government's plan for mothers' allowances when Douglas "was just a little fellow". Tommy shot back that he was "still just a little fellow and Tucker could probably swallow him for breakfast, but if he did, he'd be the strangest man in the world, having more brains in his stomach than in his head."

That story was repeated in every coffee shop in the province, even more often than the words of Tucker in the legislature when he called the Premier "a stinking skunk and a dirty little thug." Tommy only smiled and retorted that he certainly resented that "little".

As Liberal leader, Walter Tucker didn't last long. Arrogance fears nothing more than laughter. The government policy that most infuriated the Liberals and the Liberal daily newspapers was the automobile insurance program. It covered every driver and was public and compulsory, set up as a Crown corporation like Ontario Hydro Electric Power or the CBC or Trans Canada Airlines. It put several companies and private agents out of the car insurance business and substituted a single public insurer. This was an assault on "free enterprise" the Regina *Leader-Post* rumbled, a Stalinist attack on the fundamentals of free markets and "the principles of business competition". A state-run monopoly was "socialist regimentation" and would obviously be inefficient. But most of all it underlined the "communist leanings" of the CCF.

The government's case was not ideological but empirical. Every driver must have public liability insurance. Uninsured drivers are a menace, and when coverage is expensive it is not purchased by the poor or the irresponsible, but it is a must. A first principle of all insurance is that it is cheaper and more efficient if the risk is spread most widely, and if a total population is insured the premiums are lowest. This makes the insurance industry what economists call a "natural monopoly", like water supply and electric power where overlapping or duplication of service is inefficient. It is scarcely a radical view that monopolies are highly dangerous unless publicly owned or publicly regulated. Therefore the most practical solution is universal, public, compulsory, no fault auto insurance.

Whatever the arguments, the plan proved very popular. Saskatchewan soon boasted the lowest rates in the entire country, and the plan was copied in other provinces, particularly in Manitoba and British Columbia, although inexplicably the *Leader-Post* devoted little or no coverage to those developments. Many citizens chuckled a lot about the Saskatchewan Liberal newspapers posing as champions of "market competition" when they enjoyed monopoly status in the province's major cities and just for good measure owned the largest private radio (and later, TV) outlets as well. A much quoted line of Premier Douglas on the subject of "free competition" was: "We are all equal here trumpeted the elephant as he danced among the chickens."

Auto insurance was important to Jamie because on the day he turned sixteen he passed the tests for his driver's licence and the next day bought a car. It wasn't any grand vehicle, a 1929 Chev two-door, bright blue with frayed upholstery and battered front fenders. He painted the fenders red to distract from the dents and it ran very well, having been owned by a young mechanic who worked in a Texaco station nearby. It was fairly quick and nimble as long as you didn't want to drive more than 55 miles per hour. He loved the car and named it Ol' Poodadle after a character in Walt Kelly's comic strip, Pogo, his favourite. The car had cost $150, no mean sum to a student in those days. His mother had been persuaded to contribute $80 from money she'd put away for him from Family Allowance cheques and he had enough in his own bank account, earned by mowing lawns and shoveling snow and selling magazine subscriptions door to door plus $50 he'd won as first prize in a Kiwanis Club essay contest, to pay the balance and also for the licence and insurance.

The car gave him a new sense of freedom and a chance to go out with girls who didn't live near the streetcar line. For a young man few things are more uncomfortable than picking up a date for a movie and travelling by streetcar. Wheels were the big deal, any kind of wheels, and with a car you could not only go to a drive-in movie but also down by Waskana Lake and park. Since gas cost money and parking was free and the car provided privacy in the dark, he became an avid parker. In those pre-pill days 'necking' was a major backseat sport of teenagers. It was considered the height of amorous dexterity to master unhooking bra fasterners with one hand.

In fact the costs had been less of a problem than learning how to drive. That had caused trouble. At first his mother had been opposed to him learning at sixteen, which she considered too young, but slowly she relented. His father, not keen on playing the instructor, had grumpily taken him out of town on dirt back roads to give lessons. Jamie had a problem with the manual transmission. He found it balky. He let out the clutch either too slowly or too quickly, with too much or too little throttle, and every which way he tried he made the car lurch and the motor stall. This caused him to break into an embarrassed sweat and his father to shout. "No, no, more throttle, but keep it even, steady. No, no, don't race the engine like that! There, you've got it going. The gears! For god's sake don't grind the gears! Hell, you've stalled it again! Can't you—? Oh, shit! Okay, now. The ditch! Keep out of the goddamn ditch!" "I was just shifting gears." "You've gotta shift the gear without LOOKING at it AND keep out of the ditch!" I can't stand it. Enough. Stop! We're going home. Get the hell out of the way and let a man drive."

They drove home in silence.

Lorne complained to his wife that the kid was hopeless and would never learn. She asked Jamie what seemed to be the trouble.

"I get nervous. Dad shouts all the time and I get confused. It's the – disapproval, as though I'm some moron if I don't get it right the first time, and then I can't get anything right."

"Shouts? Who shouts? If he could just DO it I wouldn't have to yell at him. Do you think I want him to wreck the car?"

"Maybe if you didn't yell at him he'd get it right."

"And if he got it right I wouldn't have to yell at him. I can't stand the bloody incompetence! I've tried. I've done what I can, but no more. I give up."

"Do you want to give up, Jamie?"

"Of course not, Mom. I can do it. Just need some patience, that's all. And less shouting."

"When Roy gets back he'll help you, I'm certain. Meanwhile I'll tell you what, let's ask Uncle Milt to give you a lesson or two."

"I'd like that a whole lot, Mom."

"There you go again," the father boomed. "Milt this, Milt that. Always Milt. To hell with it! I'm going out."

And so it was arranged. With Milt's quiet and patient encouragement Jamie achieved a fair degree of competence in two lessons, real confidence in four, and everything went smoothly. A breeze.

Looking back on the incident, Jamie believed that if only Roy had been there to guide him, there'd have been no problem in the first place. Roy always knew just what to do. But now, all these three years later, where was Roy? Seldom did a day go by that he didn't think of his older brother and wonder. The biggest imponderable in uncertain situations is always "what if?" Two of his professors and the Registrar had asked Jamie if there'd been any news of Roy, any word at all? His leaving the university, his disappearance, had been so abrupt and unexplained that several people still remembered and wondered about it. Had his family ever received any useful news?

It was very melancholy to Jamie, but he was used to these inquiries and tried to deflect them. Sometimes he said they still hoped to hear from Roy soon. Sometimes he said the family thought he was in Australia and changed the subject quickly. Every time Roy's name came up he felt as though he'd been pole-axed.

For months and now years Jamie almost never failed to think of his brother before he fell asleep. Somewhere there had to be an explanation. People can't just vanish, can they? Inexplicably, yes, it seems they can. But why? Maybe the family had disappointed him somehow. Or had he, Jamie, let Roy down in some way? It's difficult to develop feelings of guilt without knowing what you might be guilty of; still, he managed it. The groping mind can raise the most improbable spectres. But surely Roy knew that his brother would make any sacrifice, do anything for him. And their dreams, like both becoming pilots, or like getting rich and buying their mother a house with a fireplace, a big stone fireplace. Could the imponderable future still permit that to happen? "Oh, Roy, do you know what anguish your absence is causing, always missing, always here?"

Jamie couldn't talk to his parents about these doubts and fears any more; they just became upset. He tried several times to articulate his feelings to his best friend, Dick Slater, but Dick only shook his head and said "There you go again", or vaguely "I guess it's different if you have a brother", and slid away from the topic. Helen Rivkin seemed more interested and sympathetic, but said very little except to ask, "What can I say?"

Helen, like everyone else in the world, had her own pre-occupations. Acting was what she most wanted to do, although even she would admit that her figure was becoming more tubby and there was a growing suggestion of a double chin . She scored a notable triumph in her drama class's Greystone Theatre presentation of *The Importance of Being Earnest* and was singled out by the local newspaper in a rave review. "Rivkin a Marvel as Lady Bracknell," enthused the *Star-Phoenix*. Dick and Jamie joined in with congratulations at the cast party afterwards, and about one a.m. Jamie boosted a case of twelve beer and drove her to a back-campus spot overlooking the river where they sat for a while in companionable silence. He opened two beers.

"Well, that's over with," Helen sighed.

"Two more nights to run, isn't it?" said Jamie.

"No, I mean that's it for my foolish career as an actress. Maybe I just had to get it out of my system. Anyhow, it's over."

"But you were wonderful, a great hit."

"Maybe."

"Yeh, yeh, the audience just loved it when you put everything into that – that trombone voice of yours and belted out, 'Found? F-o-u-n-d?' and 'In a *Handbag*??' It was great stuff, Helen, you're on your way."

"Sure," she said, lighting a cigarette, "on my way to WAY off Broadway as a bit player, a character actress, one of six or eight thousand would-be players who wait tables or pound typewriters and hope for a break that never comes. I just don't have the equipment. Don't you see it? I'm twenty years old – I should be the *ingénue*, but I'm only an age-génue, playing an old woman. Shitty pies, Jamie, I'm short and wide and dumpy. They had to make a raised part of the stage for me to stand on and teach me to walk in high platform shoes under that long skirt to give me some elevation to play Lady Bracknell. No, Tobi Weinberg has it, and Shirley Douglas has it, and Franny Hyland, too, and that's just here in Saskatchewan for pete's sake, but not me. I don't got it, and there it is."

"But Helen, for godssake, you have talent and stage presence and a great comic sense. You had the audience eating out of your hand and stole the show. I can't believe you're talking like this."

"Talking realistically. I have to face it. My career will have to be in something else. Probably journalism. I've written enough squibs for the student newspaper, *The Sheaf*, you know, and even some for the *Star-Phoenix*, so I'm pretty sure I can make a living at *something*, because it won't be acting, and probably no one will want to marry me."

"What? Whaddya mean? Any man would be *lucky* to marry you. Why, hell's bells, I'd marry you like a shot!"

Helen laughed, that deep throaty chortle, flipped her cigarette out the car window, lit another, and laughed again.

"Oh sure you would, you klutz," she said, "sure. Or maybe you might at that, but for all the wrong reasons. Our friendship is swell, but it's not like that, not at all. You're my pal and my pet, and you're younger than I am, and a sweetie and impressionable, and also just a kid who hasn't even got a B.A. yet."

"I will have, and soon, and then I'll get a law degree and Dick and I will set up in partnership together and our practice will take off like a big-assed bird. We'll make pots of money."

"Un hunh. Could be, I suppose. I can't see you joining the Rotary Club, though, to get connections and clients. Dick, maybe, but not you. I've always thought you were the brainy one of our trio, but pretty damned impatient of bullshit."

"Brains, schmains, I'm not stupid and I'm pretty good with the books, I guess, and with theory, and Dick will be a whiz at the court room stuff. We'll do just fine, you'll see. So would you marry me, when I've graduated from law and hung out my shingle, I mean, and become a success?"

"No. Not on your life. Why ruin a good friendship? Just *look* at me,

Jamie. I'm fat. I'm homely. Even my mother says I have a great face for radio." She held up a restraining hand. "Oh, now stop, do stop. You say nice things and I appreciate it, but I'm certainly no beauty, and I can't see myself as some frilly little housewife, can you? No, much as I'd like to be married some day, it's just not in the cards. I'm too loud and tough and unlovely to be some decent guy's dream of quiet domesticity."

Jamie sputtered and expostulated, but she waved a dismissive hand, then impulsively kissed him on the cheek. She leaned back in the seat, rolled down the window and lit yet another cigarette. "Damn," she laughed, "my first and maybe only marriage proposal and I can't accept it. Back to being the formidable Lady Bracknell, eh? And I guess dusting off my typewriter. Thank god it's portable, because I'll be moving on after graduation. What will you be doing?"

"Oh, not much. Another year to the B.A. and getting ready for law school. I've been having good luck with my courses in economics and pol sci, finding them more interesting than I expected, getting mostly A's on my essays, that sort of thing, I just read Harrod's biography of Maynard Keynes and I'm quite swacked by his counter-cyclical theory of how to cure depressions. Keynes is a British liberal, you know, not a socialist, but he makes a lot of sense about economic stability. What he says is ...."

"Now don't for godssake start lecturing me on economics, friend Red; I can't stand it."

"Right, okay, I won't. And reading more Peter de Vries and that new one by Salinger, you know it?"

"Yes, *Catcher in the Rye*, read it last summer. Great stuff."

"Actually I seem to be getting more into the politics side of my courses. I enjoy Norman Ward's lectures the most. He's been, well, encouraging me and talking about helping find me a scholarship if I want to go on to post-grad work. He's a really great guy, Helen, even took me out duck hunting with him last fall."

"Did you shoot anything?"

"Aw, you know I wouldn't do that. Professor Ward has two shotguns and gave me his old one and sent me down to the other end of the marsh to take a few shots at anything that came my way. One stupid Mallard flew right at me and I had to fire away to the left to avoid hitting him but to make it look like I tried. I guess I'd never make much of a hunter. I liked it better in the early fall when Norm let me come out to the golf course with him and his friend Des Conacher, just to caddy, and then we went to the Princess and they bought me a couple of beers."

"Speaking of which, open me another, will you?"

"Sure. Here you go."

"So is Professor Ward your new father figure?"

"Hm? How do you mean?"

"I mean father figure like you had with that English teacher Jed Howard in high school."

"Hey, wait, I loved old Jed and I really like Dr. Ward, but I wouldn't put it like *that*."

"I would. It's plain as the nose on your face that you don't much get on with your own Dad and are always looking for a substitute, what do you call it, a surrogate father. The thing is, and it's not necessarily a bad thing, you're a bit of a softie, Jamie, and for all your smarts and your happy personality, you seem not to be as hard or independent as Dick is, or I am, more dependent, prob'ly expecting too much of people. No, no, I don't mean just wet puppyish, but too eager to please and not, I'd say, overly self-reliant, self-confidant. First your brother, then Mr. Howard, now Dick, or Dr. Ward. You love praise and who doesn't, but maybe you need it more than most, and you get attached to people you really like and you're a little too ready to sell yourself short and do what they want you to do. Don't you realize how good you are, how bright? Just as yourself?"

"Gosh, Helen, I've never thought about it like that. I mean, I guess I'm pretty good and all, but ...."

"So, friend Red, while we're getting it a bit more sorted out, let me tell you something else."

"Shit, what's next?"

"Let me try this on. What will you do if Dick backs out on you and doesn't do law? Then what would you do?"

"Doesn't do law? But we've always planned on it! Why in hell would you say a thing like that?"

"Just asking. What would you do?"

"Buggered if I know. That's such a leap in the dark. Why, has Dick said anything about that to you? This can't be right. You've gotta tell me what he's said."

"Nothing much, in all truth, nothing definite, but I'm trying to put two and two together and I've got this feeling that it doesn't add up. I'd hate to see you disappointed, that's all."

"Evidence," said Jamie, reaching for two more beers. "What sort of evidence, what sort of feeling? Are you just having me on for the hell of it or is there something you're trying to tell me? Lay it out, Helen, please, or at least say what's got you thinking this way or I can't take you seriously, damn it."

"I'm telling you, or trying to tell you, that no, he's said nothing directly to me, some little hints only. But I don't believe he's serious about law school. I don't. He's so wrapped up in the student politics thing that he's letting his grades slide. He may not have the marks to get into law, and he doesn't seem to care. He'd need Latin, too, for entrance, and he hasn't got it. No Latin, no grades, no admission. Do you see it?"

"Shit, it only takes Grade 12 Latin, like I've got, and he can pick that up, take a summer school course easy enough. That's no big deal."

"And has he taken it? He's already had to do one summer school course to make up French because he cut classes and flunked it. Doesn't help his average much. But no Latin. If he were serious about law he'd be serious about entrance requirements, don't you think? All I'm saying is, don't count on Dick. Don't count on anyone. Except yourself. Or else you could be left dangling. If you want to bet on it, I'll give you two-to-one that he won't take law. And you'll be sentimental about it, and he won't. Self-preservation is what it's all about, I'd say. Now, I've got to get out for a minute and have a pee in the bushes. Hold my beer, will you?"

Jamie took the bottle and swigged and sat and thought about it, feeling incredulous, feeling like a shattered light bulb. None of these possibilities had ever occurred to him. His mind raced and tumbled.

When Helen climbed back into the car she patted his knee and said, "I may be wrong, Sort of hope I am, but I don't think so. I'm only trying to protect you. Just think about it. You might need a back-up plan, as I do. An alternative."

"Damned if I know what I'd do. Some of my profs have made suggestions, but I've never taken them all that seriously. Look, if you're right, and I'm not ready to say you are, I could make it on my own in law, join an established practice, settle down here in Saskatoon and have a good life. For sure I could."

"But is that what you'd really want?"

"Sounds pretty good to me. Look, kiddo, are you trying to freak me out? Trying to make me feel bad? Because you've run up against a disappointment yourself? That might be understandable, but it's not like you, Helen."

"Nope, it's not that. And, I admit I'm not sure, although I've been thinking about it for a while. Consider it only an amber light or warning, not a stop sign." She paused and drank and lit another weed. "Another thing I'll admit is that I've always liked Dick, always will, and sometimes I think I'm half in love with the silly bastard myself. I wonder why we're always drawn to the oddballs? That unpredictable roguish charm really works for him, particularly with women, and I can be as susceptible as apparently you are, but could I really trust him? Can you? I think he'll go his own way, probably an erratic but jaunty way, no matter what you or I might want or expect. Now, for all that, shall we call it a night—Jeez, it's after 3 a.m.—and drive me home? Stars of the stage and screen like me and Rita Hayworth need our beauty sleep." She laughed and patted his knee again.

He started the car and backed out to the road, still more than somewhat confused and worried. As he drove he continued to muse and mutter.

"It's the river, I think. It always makes me wonder and speculate about – life, does it you? Mesmerizing. 'Dat ol' man ribber', as Robeson sings it. Flows like time, flows like destiny itself."

"Oh, stop it, Jamie."

"No, I mean it. Whenever I sit by the river I seem to blot out yesterday and think more clearly. It calms me and makes me feel more easy and more happy, even if we're pondering upsetting questions like tonight's. It's what Regina doesn't have, and it makes all the difference to Saskatoon. And the bridges. The river just flows and draws me to it, makes me feel part of nature and more connected to the universe. I've often thought that when I make enough money practising law here – maybe – I'd build a house on a hill overlooking the river and just gaze at it and be, um, content."

"You do get carried away. Although I will say it's one thing I'll miss when I move on out of here."

"Where will you go, do you think?"

"Wherever I can find the right kind of job, I suppose. Vancouver, maybe back to the 'States, or even east, to Toronto. Not to any small town, though. I'm going to travel, and aim high. And you? Where would you go? Have you begun to think of alternatives to Saskatoon and the river?"

"Not really, no. It will all work out. Maybe graduate school, like Ward suggests, if a scholarship really comes through. The chairman of my department recently gave me the notion of staying here for an M.A. and sitting the exams for External Affairs, you know, foreign service officer, diplomat, travel, striped trousers and cocktail parties."

"God knows you're nothing if not diplomatic. But the catch might be, you have no control over where they'd send you."

"Would that matter?"

"Might. Hold it, stop here, you almost drove past my apartment. But haven't I ever told you about my friend Joan who married into the foreign service? No? Well, Joan is older than I am and studied law and married her law prof. Thought she'd settled down. But External Affairs kept trying to recruit her husband because of his specialty in international law. He hesitated, but they told him he'd be posted to only the best places: London, Washington, Paris, maybe Rome .... So he signed on. The thing was, they stuck him in Ottawa for two years and still no posting. Finally his boss called him in one morning and said, 'Well, Smith, Karachi.' And he smiled and replied. 'Gesundheit.' Ain't bureaucracy grand? He went, though, and actually enjoyed it, and seems to be having a good career. So think about that, and think about what I've said. I'm gonna fall into bed. G'night, and thanks for the beer."

"Gesundheit, Helen."

"Karachi, Jamie. Sleep well."

XIII

Since he'd been away at university for three years Jamie had always made a point of writing to his parents once a week. Nothing very newsy, just brief accounts of what he was doing, what he was reading, reports that he was well fed in the residence dining hall, occasional chat about Dick and Helen. These "Dear Mom and Dad" missives always prompted a quick reply from his mother who brooded over him like a hen with only a solitary chick. She prattled on about Regina gossip which interested him not in the least, or about his Dad's firm opinions concerning provincial politics which Jamie found obtuse and ill informed at best.

Lately, two, almost three weeks had gone by without even a note from his mother. He wasn't worried, rather relieved in fact about a break in the shuttlecock correspondence, but decided to spend a couple of bucks phoning home. His mother twittered that everything was fine, she was fine, only she'd had rather an embarrassing fall down the back steps causing a few bruises which she called "minor" and a sprained wrist which made writing "uncomfortable".

"Look, Mom, I've got a few days off school pretty soon, spring break, a week, almost ten days between the end of classes and the beginning of exams, so I'll come home for a short visit. Have you been to a doctor?"

"Well, no, I don't see the need for a doctor or to spend money pointlessly. I'm fine, really. Don't bother coming if it's not convenient with your schoolwork and everything."

"It's okay. All my essays and term work are in, and I'll bring a few books with me. I'm pretty much up on my work."

"How would you come down, dear? Not in that little old car, I hope. And not by hitchhiking like that—that other time, you hear?"

"Yes, Mom. I'll take the bus. Doesn't cost much. Is Uncle Milt likely to be around?"

"He's been away on another business trip, in the east, I think, maybe Toronto, maybe Ottawa. I never remember."

"Maybe I'll see him later. So, you can expect me, let's see, a week from Wednesday, okay?"

"That would be nice, dear."

The arrangement, in fact, was not all that convenient to him with exams coming up, but he hadn't seen his parents since December. Christmas had not been entirely jolly. Roy's absence was keenly felt but never mentioned. Uncle Milt was not with them, being away in Hawaii with his latest girlfriend (Jean said he was 'shamefully promiscuous') and not available to leaven the family lump. This disappointed Jamie because he no longer regarded Milt as just an uncle but as a close friend, and he depended on his friends a lot. Who was it that said, friends are the gods' compensation for relatives?

So it was only the three McRaes who quietly performed the ritual exchange of ties and shirts and socks around a small Christmas tree. Milt had wired a bouquet of flowers to Jean, and Jamie gave his mother some not very expensive perfume that Helen had helped him choose. Lorne's gift to his wife was a vacuum cleaner. "Hope you like it," he smiled; "you said you needed a new one."

They sat down to dinner at the table where Jean had arranged her best Spode china, a wedding gift from her parents, around a red poinsettia, and festive Yuletide paper napkins rolled in silver rings, a gift from her brother. His father nursed a small tumbler of rye and water by his plate. He'd offered one to Jamie, who declined. The meal was a dry overdone turkey, cranberry sauce, turnips, and vivid molds of lime Jell-O with carrot shreds and niblet corn imbedded in them. Jamie smiled and smiled and repeatedly said "mmm" and wished they could send out for a pizza. It seemed odd that there was not even music in the house to bridge the frequent silences, and belatedly he remembered that his parents had never owned a record player.

He hoped this spring visit would be less depressing.

This time his father was not at home when he arrived. He thought his mother's face had visibly aged over the past four months, the corners of her mouth set more downward and fixed. Wrinkles were deepening around her eyes, and she seemed pale and vaguely distracted. She kept asking if he'd brought laundry and, assured that he hadn't, made a fuss about changing the sheets on his bed.

"Why bother, Mom? Has someone been sleeping in it?"

"No, no, just me. Occasionally."

"And why is that, Mom?"

"No reason. Just sometimes to get more rest, you know? I get so tired these days, so very tired."

"Why not sleep in Roy's bed?"

"Oh, I couldn't bring myself to do *that*."

"Uh hunh. I guess I know what you mean. But still you've gotta have sleep."

"The truth is, your father has been drinking a bit again."

"A bit?"

"Well, quite a bit. Sometimes. I find it – trying."

"Any reason?"

"Isn't there always a reason? He found out that your Uncle Milt had invested in that big motel a few years back, and he was, um, envious about how profitable it is and cursed a lot. Last winter your father had some more bad luck with that sort of thing. Apparently he'd put some money, he never told me how much, into a mine with a friend, a copper mine in the north up near Lac La Rouge. But it didn't work out."

"Should I be surprised?"

"I suppose not. No copper. And soon, no friend."

"Damn. He's always had a remarkable knack for getting in on the ground floor of castles in the sky. It must drive you bananas."

"Oh, he means well, dear. He's always tried hard, and dreams of having real money. And if he got ahead financially, with even one good investment, he'd spend money on us, on you and on me. He'd buy a house, and maybe a new car for you. He would. You know that. He's a good man. Just unlucky."

"Sure, Mom, I know that. It's okay. Some day his ship might come in. I hope so. Meanwhile, I won't hold my breath."

"There's always hope, Jamie. We must have faith. Come along, then. Your dinner is ready."

They chatted idly through an indifferent meal of pork chops with apple jelly and green peas from a can. Lorne had not yet returned. Over a dish of vanilla ice cream for dessert, Jamie said he might turn in early with a book. He made an exaggerated yawn and kissed his mother goodnight.

A noise in the living room wakened him about one a.m. Loud voices in the living room. He sat up in bed and rubbed his eyes and listened. His dad was back. His dad was drunk.

"You're all beered up again. Jamie is here. You'll have to sleep on the couch."

"I'm not sleeping on any damn couch! A working man needs his rest."

"Working, is it? And just where might you have been working tonight, and the night before? This is the first time you've deigned to come home in two days. A grand family man you are, I must say."

"You always 'must have your say'," he muttered, mimicking her. "Does it matter where I've been? I've been busy. Tonight I was trying to sell a man a road grader. He's a tough sell. Last night was a poker game with some construction engineers I deal with. Game went on till dawn and I didn't feel right leaving while I was ahead."

"Do I dare hope that you were still ahead when you did leave?"

"Not then, no. Maybe down a little, a few bucks, but one of the boys took an I.O.U. marker. No problem."

"There's never any problem with you, is there? Just the same old facts of booze and money that always come home to me. Always the same!"

"Not always," he mumbled, and started toward the bedroom with only a small lurch.

Jean flared. "I can't stand it! This is more than I can bear! You're an awful husband, just awful. You give me a miserable life, and I will *not* put up with any more of this!" She was screaming. "Why can't we have a proper life, like other people? Why can't I have a decent life? What have I ever done to deserve this?"

Weeping, she gave him a push and while he was off balance began to hit at his shoulders with her tiny fists. He turned and held her away. Frantically she continued to weep and wail and tried to beat on his chest. Jamie, fully awake now, ran swiftly to the living room. Just before he came around the door he heard a thump, then found his mother sprawled in a chair.

"Mom! Where did he hit you?"

She shook her head and sobbed.

"I never hit her, she hit me and I gave her a shove. She's all right, just hysterical about nothing, the silly bitch."

"Don't you call my mother a bitch!" He took an angry swing at his father who saw it coming and warded off the punch with a burly forearm. Jamie clipped him on the ear with a left, then tried another roundhouse swing with a right which Lorne caught with his hand. The standoff was interrupted by a piercing cry from Jean.

"Stop it," she yelled through tears. "Stop it at once, both of you!"

"Stop what?" Lorne growled. "There's nothing *to* stop. Bloody kid can't even throw a proper punch."

"You hit your father!" she screeched again. "You raised your hand against your own father! You struck him!"

"But – but Mom, I was only trying to help you, defend you. I mean – I mean I was only – are you all right? Are you hurt?"

"Of course I'm all right! Everything's *perfect*. I've got a drunken husband and a son who attacks his father and a fistfight in my living room in the middle of the night. I never could have imagined such a thing. I'm ashamed of you, Jamie. Tell your father that you're sorry."

"Ashamed of *me*? Sorry? I'm sure as hell not sorry. I wish I'd smacked him a good one."

"Enough!" she shouted. "That's quite enough out of both of you! I've never been so horrified in my life. A couple of brawlers in my own house. Get out of my sight, both of you, before I phone for the police, or the neighbours do. Go to bed. Get to bed now before I'm mortified any further."

"But Mom ...."

"Now, I say. Go to bed and say nothing more that we'll all regret tomorrow."

In the morning Lorne rose early, took a shot of vodka to steady his hangover, and left the house in silence.

When Jamie got up, much later, and ate a breakfast of Grape Nuts Flakes, milk, and coffee, the atmosphere was heavy. His mother barely spoke and wouldn't look him in the eye.

"I'm sorry you had such a rough night of it, Mom."

"Don't tell me," she snapped, "tell your father. Apologize."

"Tell him I'm sorry? Apologize to *him*? No. I can't, I won't."

"Ah, well then. If you won't I expect you'll find dinner here tonight rather dreary."

"Uh hunh. Maybe I should just pack and go back up to the university."

"Oh, Jamie, don't do that. Stay if you want to. Please."

"It might be best if I left. Exams and all, you know."

"It's a shame."

"Yes, it is. But tell me, after seeing that dust–up last night, did your sprained wrist and 'minor' bruises last month really happen because of an accident on the stairs, or did Dad have something to do with that?"

"What?" She paused. "You don't know what you're saying! No, nothing like that, no, of course not."

"You're not going to tell me, are you?"

"There's nothing to tell. Nothing. Certainly not."

But still she would not meet his eyes. He thought that his once pretty and vibrant mother now appeared drab and disconsolate.

On the bus ride north he mulled the situation over and over but decided there was nothing he could do. His mother seemed abjectly resigned, as though she'd given up on everything. It distressed him ineffably that the bright dancing eyes were now clouded and dull, the hope and vitality drained out of them. But he knew that after almost thirty years of living together in an unfortunate marriage two people will inevitably do what they must do, be what they've become.

What a lousy trip, he thought. He decided to look for a summer job in Saskatoon.

XIV

Although Dick and Helen had entered university ahead of Jamie, he soon caught up with them. Helen decided to stay on campus one more year as editor of *The Sheaf*, its first female editor, and caught on with the *Star-Phoenix* in a part-time job in the Women's Section. Important experience, she said, given that women were still regarded as second class citizens in the newsroom.

She had been proven right about Dick Slater. He had given up on entering law school. His grades had slipped, he admitted, and there didn't seem much point to trying a Latin class. Instead he enrolled in the Faculty of Education, saying he intended to be a high school teacher. This gravely disappointed Jamie. Two months earlier Dick's decision would have sliced him like a scythe but Helen's warning had shielded him. Now he saw a door closing, but also an alternative door opening to graduate studies in economics.

Ironically it was his final experience as a debater that showed him a new and different field to investigate. Dick had talked him into one more crack at inter-collegiate debating, and although he was reluctant to take time from course work, he agreed to be Dick's partner in responding to a challenge from the University of Alberta team which they'd previously defeated. Mainly he didn't want to let his friend down, but the proposed topic also appealed to him: 'Resolved – That Canada should have a National Health Insurance scheme similar to that of Great Britain.' The more he read about his subject the more absorbed he became.

Helen's father, Dr. Abe Rivkin, sent along some articles and literature for the boys to read, plus an extended bibliography on health care to be perused as time permitted. The boys were surprised by the quantity of material available. It became apparent that there was no single uniform scheme of public health insurance. Germany, France, Israel, Sweden and the U.K. all displayed different and varied arrangements, but all agreed on universal coverage.

Whenever Jamie bogged down under the mass of information he'd sit back and remember his father fulminating on the subject: Medicare would be far too expensive, create political control through a huge state bureaucracy, and lead to low standards of homogenous service. These were, amusingly enough, exactly the same arguments used in the nineteenth century against universal public education. And to muster his arguments on the positive side all he had to ask himself was: How would the Premier put it? What would Tommy say? And that became his chief criterion and moral compass.

The rules of debate at that time were that each team would prepare to defend both sides of the resolution, affirmative and negative, with the side to be taken determined by the toss of a coin by the debate judge one hour before the contest began. This was intended to reduce any reliance on formally written or memorized speeches, and to promote spontaneity. Luckily the coin toss gave the University of Saskatchewan the affirmative and Jamie, in particular (although he was careful to emphasize "similar" to the British plan, not identical), was able to launch a spirited plea for universal public health insurance or 'Medicare' as a right and a necessity in a civilized country. After Dick spoke with his characteristic verve and wit, Jamie surprised even himself with the conviction and passion he brought to his final rebuttal on the need for Medicare, and they won the debate handily. What pleased Jamie even more was that he had found a subject within the realm of economics and the social sciences about which he could be genuinely excited.

He soon learned that it would be no easy path to become a health economist. Conversations with his professors confirmed what he had found in various graduate school calendars; there were no graduate programs or even courses in the economics of health in any Canadian university. Dr. Rivkin, consulted later when he was in Saskatoon visiting Helen, said he was not at all surprised, for there were damn few courses like that in American universities either. In Britain, however, there was a professor, Brian Abel-Smith, at the London School of Economics who'd published a lot in the field and whom Dr. Rivkin (call me 'Abe') could recommend very highly. Jamie was grateful and said he'd look up the works of Abel-Smith in the library as soon as possible.

"One other thing," said Abe, "because you're obviously interested and a friend of Helen's, I'll tell you in confidence—don't run to any newspaper with this—our Tommy has strongly indicated that he's committed to some form of Medicare and intends to make Saskatchewan the leader and pioneer in this field as soon as possible. There's no doubt in my mind that we'll be the first province in all of Canada, in all of North America for that matter, to establish public health insurance. He's already asked me and others in the Department of Health, and my friend Tom Shoyama, the head of the Economic Advisory and Planning Board, to start preparing cost estimates and feasibility studies. Shoy is a very canny fellow, solid and dependable, who's already read all the material I've given you in that bibliography, and he's very good at sorting out the comparative international lessons in health care delivery." Abe chuckled. "You've gotta get up real early and think damned fast to get ahead of Shoy. Or ahead of Premier Douglas, I'd say."

Jamie beamed at him and thanked Abe cordially for his time and help.

"Oh, and let me tell you this too," Abe added. "I'll offer a prediction, and don't quote me on this either. When Medicare legislation is introduced here, there'll be one helluva battle, one flaming big brouhaha that will shake the rafters and test this government. A political firestorm. You think the right wing opposition kicked up a fuss about public auto insurance? All that 'Tucker or tyranny' and 'free enterprise über alles' nonsense? As we say in New York, boychik, you ain't seen nuthin' yet."

When Jamie related Abe's words to his two friends, Helen was skeptical. "Oh that's just my dad being dramatic and alarmist. I can't believe that the doctors or even the Liberals would get the wind up like that. Dad's just being your typical Bronx radical, always believing the worst of what the right wingers will get up to, always looking for a fight. I wouldn't take him too seriously."

"I would," said Dick. "Never underestimate the power of the insurance industry and big business. This new Liberal opposition leader, Ross Thatcher, is a tough cookie and not just all bluster like Tucker was. If Thatcher can persuade the doctors, even most of the well meaning non-political doctors, that the CCF is truly Red and a threat to free enterprise, then he could put up an awful nasty fight. My political instincts may be better than yours, certainly more cynical, and I'd say that what Thatcher might do is build a really big and rough anti-CCF organization, maybe defeat the government with a Red scare on the health issue, and then do the classic Liberal thing of adopting and adapting socialist policy ideas, making them his own, and then sweet talking the big interests into accepting his version of health insurance—which is certain to be popular, our debating stuff showed us that—and after dressing it up in new clothes, bring it in as his own creation a few years after he gets in to power. Let the CCF take the lumps as dangerous radicals, and then take the credit for the whole schemmozle."

"Shitty pies, Dick, you certainly *are* a cynic," said Helen with a shake of her head.

"Bloody right," Jamie agreed.

"Cynical? I'd just say 'realist'," Dick replied. "But look at it historically. We learned this from our debating material. Who was it started the Medicare thing in Europe in the first place? Some commie? Hardly. It was ...."

"Otto von Bismarck," Jamie muttered. "The Iron Chancellor of Germany, the Prussian, in the 1880s to outflank the Reds. I hadn't thought of it like that. I see what you mean. He might be right, Helen."

"Damn straight, I am. All this 'radical' thing is a crock anyway. Do you remember how Ambrose Bierce defined 'radicalism' in his *Devil's Dictionary*? It was you, Helen, who gave me that book. He defined radicalism as 'The conservativism of tomorrow injected into the affairs of today.' Not bad, that. All a matter of perspective, smoke and mirrors."

"Could be," said Jamie, "but I'd never bet against Tommy. If anyone can pull it off, he can."

"We'll see," Dick said. "Maybe."

XV

After the B.A. in 1954 Jamie McRae received an M.A. in economics in 1955, as far as he could go in that discipline in Saskatchewan. Helen Rivkin had departed the previous year to the west coast and a job with the *Vancouver Sun*, where she quickly rose from the Women's Section to become a political reporter. Dick Slater, having spent one jaunty year as president of the Students' Council and another catching up with his work in the College of Education, added a B.Ed. to his B.A. and started looking for a teaching job.

Luckily money became less of a problem for Jamie. Two summers' work on the line at Drewry's brewery, with a lot of overtime in the hot thirsty weather, had earned him a small savings account while he lived frugally. He'd received a small monthly stipend of $40 during his last year as a marking assistant for Norman Ward's big freshman class, and was awarded two scholarships to pursue a Ph.D. One, a Sanderson Fellowship, was for a year in the U.K. at the London School of Economics; the other for an alternate year was a Canada Council grant, possibly renewable, to study at the University of Toronto. The question was, which one to take up first? The year in London seemed enticing. Ward said it didn't much matter. Jamie decided to consult with Uncle Milt.

"Yes, by all means do the year in London first," said Milt. "It will do you a power of good. You can do the Toronto degree later, after a fling at Europe. By god, that will set you up and shake you up. You've yet to become a traveler, and to wipe the prairie dust off your boots will give you a new lease on life, a new perspective. Just think of it: England, maybe Paris, possibly even Rome or Florence or … damned if I don't think I'm talking myself into coming over to visit while you're there. We could cut a wide swath through the pubs and bistros, eh, Jamie me lad? *Pâté de fois gras* for two, m'sieur!"

"Now wait, Milt, let's not get carried away. I have a bit of money saved from summer work, but nothing like enough to live high on the hog in fancy restaurants. Besides, I'll have work to do at the London School. They don't hand out Ph.D. credits for pub crawling. Those scholarships, remember, are only enough to cover the basics."

"Oh I know, I know, but with the M.A. in your pocket you've earned a bit of a lark, a break and a holiday, a few rewards. I'm just so damn proud that you've done so well. You've everything to look forward to."

"Thanks. Yes, it's exciting. I'm glad you're pleased – Maybe my parents are, too."

"No doubt about it. And look, I want to tell you one other thing. I think you realize that a bachelor like me, with not much need to spend money on things, has more loose change and more in the bank than your parents have. I slipped a few extra bucks to Roy when he first went off to university, but then your mother and Lorne made me promise not to overdo it, not to spoil you boys, so I've had to hold back all this time. I think maybe Lorne was afraid of being upstaged. But now we might bend that promise, change the rules some. So here's what I propose."

Milt shifted his chubby cigar and stared at the ceiling as though considering the situation for the first time, although in fact he'd been thinking about it for weeks.

"We won't make a lot of noise about this to your parents—agreed?— but here's the deal. I'll pony up some dollars for your train ticket to Montreal and for passage, return of course, on a ship to England, probably Cunard to Liverpool and British Rail to London. Then you won't have to spend scholarship money till you get there. Sounds okay so far?"

"Okay? It sounds wonderful, marvelous! I can't tell you, I mean, Jeez, that's *so* generous and I …."

"Wait, wait, there's one other thing I have in mind that I think might work. Let me finish a thought here. Because you and your friend Dick have been buddies since high school, almost inseparable, and I like him too, I thought you might both be pleased if I stretched the deal just a bit to *two* tickets so he could go along with you. Tickets only, you understand, no big deal, but it occurred to me that with this B.Ed. he could easily get jobs part-time in London as a supply teacher, as much or as little work as he wants to keep himself in fish and chips while you're studying, and at holiday time you could do some travelling together for what they used to call 'the conventional scamper on the Continent'. How does that sound? You think he'd like that? And you would?"

"Like it? He'd love it! We both would! That's simply great, Milt, bloody grand. You're sure we wouldn't be tapping your resources too much? I mean, that's truly a helluva pile of money and …."

"Nope. Easiest thing in the world, and my pleasure. Consider it done. I had a bit of money set aside for Roy anyway, as well as for you, and now it looks as though, ah, he won't be using it for a while. I've already sounded out Dick's dad on this to tell the truth, and he seemed more than pleased, delighted in fact. I told him, and you can tell Dick, that I made an unexpected bundle on the stock market recently, and that's true too, and I can't really think of a better use for a few surplus bucks than to receive post cards from you two from the Champs-Elysées."

"Milt, this is fantastic. It's impossible to thank you enough. I'm – I'm overwhelmed. Dick will be too. This is just the greatest thing that's ever happened to me! You old fox, you've been thinking about this for quite a while, haven't you? It's all so wonderful."

"It's only money, me boy. This is a great satisfaction to me. You're a great satisfaction, always have been, so I'm glad to be able to do it. Now get on with it, and go and tell Dick."

Jamie phoned the Slater house in Regina later that evening, but Dick wasn't in. His dad made a lot of cordial remarks about the Silver Fox, said he'd let Jamie break the news himself, and said Dick would be in Saskatoon the next day for some National Students' council meeting. "Tell him to meet me at the Empire for a beer about five, or to phone me if some other hour is better."

At five the following day they lined up some glasses of beer on a stained and wet table of the Empire Hotel's 'licenced premises', Jamie twitching with excitement and thinking how soon their lives would change and they'd be drinking British ale in a London pub. Dick wanted to talk about his summer job in a gas station and about a new girlfriend named Linda, but Jamie couldn't wait and cut him off.

"I've got news, Dick, tremendous news. Listen to this!"

Dick, who never liked being interrupted, listened, sipping his beer thoughtfully. Jamie blurted out the whole story, his words tumbling along in an enthusiastic torrent.

"Well, there it is, all laid on! Isn't that splendid? It's bloody marvelous, don't you think? You haven't said a word. Some surprise, eh? Say something."

Dick's face remained placid. He tipped up his glass of beer, drank deeply, and signaled to a waiter. Several seconds clicked off on the bar's clock.

"So your Uncle Milt wants to play God, is that it? Arrange people's lives with a flash of his cheque book. I guess that doesn't work for me."

"Doesn't work? What? You mean … oh, Milt doesn't expect anything from you, or even from me. He's just creating this great opportunity for us, the chance of a lifetime. A gift! A wildly generous gift. Can't you see us, strolling down the Strand, sitting in the gallery of the House of Commons, climbing the Tower of London? I mean, it will be fabulous. Hey, Dicky-Richard, we'll have an absolute blast. We'll book passage right away for early September …. Why in the flaming hell are you shaking your head? Don't you believe it yet?"

"Oh, I believe it all right, for you, but not for me. No. I'm not going."

"What? What are you saying? You're joshing, right? Having me on?"

"Nope. Sorry. Can't do it."

Jamie gaped at him, incredulous.

"It sounds pretty good, I'll admit, but it would be a lot of trouble."

"Trouble? What trouble for kristssake?"

"Well, for one thing, I'm not keen to be a supply teacher in some London slum. For another, I've just signed a contract for next year, not for a village or a small town, but to teach in a city, a very good position, in Prince Albert. It's what I want. I'll start after Labour Day."

"Prince Albert? Prince bloody Albert? Instead of London? I can't believe you're serious. There's plenty of time to cancel that contract, postpone it for a year, they can get a quick replacement. Shit, you gotta get real, you gotta come. Look, London, Paris, maybe, I don't know, Amsterdam, any goddamn place in Europe you want."

"Nope. I don't want. Travel doesn't much appeal to me, as I guess it does to you. Simple as that. It's no go. Lots of luck to you, and I hope you enjoy all that international shitteroo, but count me out. It's just not me."

Jamie was rendered speechless, dissolved into a puddle of disbelief.

"Anyhow, enough of this chatter," said Dick calmly. "Let's blow this joint and walk up to the Patricia Café and get something to eat. I missed my lunch on the bus up. I'll tell you about Linda. Now *there's* news. You'll like her. I'm thinking of marrying her. That would be better than some never-never land across the goddamn ocean, I'd say."

"And I'd say you're nuts, out of your fucking skull." He looked at Dick wide-eyed, as if he'd never seen him before. Odd how you can know someone, maybe all your life, and still be mystified by them.

That night Jamie scribbled a hasty note to Helen to tell her about the offer and Dick's rejection of it. Unbelievable, he wrote. As he flopped into bed he ran through a few lines of Kipling's 'If' as often he did. 'If neither foes nor loving friends can hurt you, If all men count with you, but none too much.' And sighed, and with an even sharper pang of regret thought of Roy. Would he spend the rest of his life alone, missing closest friends so acutely? Confused and despondent, finally he slept.

Helen wrote back quickly.

> *Dear Jamie,*
>
> *No, not unbelievable. Weird and wrong-headed, I think, but entirely credible. I told you, two years ago, not to count on him, didn't I? Neither you nor I can hear that different rigid and confining drummer, but that's all he marches to. Strange, but there it is. With Dick, always expect the unexpected. He seems to have a certain crazy wisdom that works for him but makes little sense to me.*
>
> *I'm sorry he won't go, but more for his sake than yours. It's still a golden opportunity, and I believe some day he'll regret it, while I'm sure you'll make the most of it. As the farmer said, trying to coax his old truck up the hill, 'give 'er snoose!'*
>
> *Go grab it, my friend. Trust yourself. Gesundheit.*
>
> *Much love,*
>
> *Helen*
>
> *P.S. I'm sending a note to Dick, giving him the inestimable benefit of my thoughts. Also find enclosed an address and phone number for my friend Ellie Jensen who's just moved from Vancouver to London with the **Daily Express**. She's a bright and lovely girl and zippy. You'll like her.*

Jamie put in as much overtime as he could at the brewery and beefed up his savings. He had to spend some time arranging passage on the Empress of Britain, getting a passport and shots, buying a second hand steamer trunk and a suitcase, and reading guidebooks to London and to British pubs. He arranged that Dick would drive his old Chev up to Prince Albert, try to sell it there and send along any money it fetched.

His last trip home to see his parents before his departure was no more happy or enspiriting than his previous visit. His father's face seemed set in a grim impassivity, his body thicker and more flabby. He seldom spoke except in rumbling monosyllables or terse imprecations against stupid governments or oppressive taxation. The face of his mother was more gray and careworn, her hair more wispy and there were two dark moles on her thin neck. What he remembered from years gone by as her bright eyes, asking and hopeful, were now dull and accepting, defeated. It pained him to see her looking so drawn and old. The pain was made more acute by his realization that there was nothing he could do about it. Time and the weather run backwards for no one.

Jamie thought there was something much more cheerful in his mother's announcement in a letter a month ago that dad had actually bought a piece of land. Not a house, but one hundred feet of shoreline on Lake Katepwa at Sandy Point. They were going to build on it next summer. Just a modest cabin, Jean now explained, although they could add on to it in the future, and there'd be a fireplace, just a small one, a little metal Acorn open firebox, but it would give heat and a pretty glow of burning logs. Later on they could build a real fireplace of bricks or even stone, with a hearth. Wouldn't that be nice?

"It sounds real good," said Jamie, trying to sound more enthusiastic than he was and wishing that there'd been such a cottage when he and Roy were boys. "Was it expensive?"

"Not a bit," said his father. "The rural municipality had foreclosed for back taxes, and the clerk tipped me off to it in return for a cheap used road grader I found for him. Got it for a song. It's down near a creek. Trees a bit sparse. Has a good sand beach, though."

"Isn't your father clever, dear? Our own piece of land."

"Great. Have you got drawings, a plan for it? Who will build it?"

"Build the summbitch myself. Not hard. My friend Lyle Gardiner agreed to help me, and then I'll help him with his place."

"Has he bought land too? On the same lake?" Jean asked.

"Yup, right next door to us. Real handy."

"Beside us? Eunice Gardiner just isn't my kind. She's so — common. We'll never really get along."

"You will. She's fine. They're grateful to me for selling them the land."

"How do you mean? We don't have any to sell."

"Sold Lyle half of our lot. Fifty feet."

"Lorne, you didn't. You didn't! Fifty feet isn't enough, not enough for either of us, except maybe for a small place, a shack. You've ruined it all, ruined everything!"

"Oh, we'll each have our bit of beach front, that's what counts. Lyle's happy. I'm happy. Nice to have such friends close by."

"*Too* close," Jean wailed. "Much too close. We'll have no privacy at all."

"Enough."

"And the Gardiners have three kids still in school. Too many for a small place. Think of the noise! We'll be overrun."

Into the following silence Jamie inserted: "I guess I'm still in school, too, and I'm not noisy."

"Oh, you," muttered his father, "the perpetual student living off the taxpayers, in pursuit of some Ph.D. or other in socialist mumbo-jumbo or economics or whatever you call it."

"Is that what you think, Dad? Really?"

"I do, yup. Why don't you get a job and earn a living like a grownup instead of traipsing all over the world studying radical crap like the Communist Manifesto?"

"Lorne, Lorne, stop it at once," cried Jean. "You've spoiled our plans for the cottage and sold off our land to those – those people, and now you're attacking Jamie for nothing, our Jamie who hasn't cost you a penny for years."

"I pay taxes don't I? Does he? That's what's wrong with this world, freeloaders. I think I'll go out for a while."

"Lorne McRae, you're not going anywhere. You'll listen to me if you know what's good for you. Now apologize to Jamie this instant."

"For what? Nope. I guess I do get carried away a bit, but I'm just as entitled to speak my piece as the next guy. Some family, this, I must say. I make a couple of bucks on real estate and suddenly I'm all wrong and anything I say is wrong, just because I have common sense and understand about business and nobody else around here does. That makes me an ogre, does it?"

Beside herself with disappointment and anger, Jean launched into a recital of grievances and complaints, some old, some recent, all bitter. "Haven't I told you and told you? .... Didn't I warn you? ...." "Yeah, yeah." "And that time that you ....?" "Can't you just knock it off, woman, can't you just forget it?"

But little was forgotten as they trotted out the old sad litany of frustrations and recriminations, nothing omitted on either side of the barbed wire fence between them where each had hoarded up charges and countercharges to be lobbed into the argument like hand grenades, certain to wound and maim. Jamie, having heard it all before, stumbled out of the room and took refuge in bed with a book, their voices still echoing in his ears. He knew from long and wretched experience that they'd continue to slash and shout at each other until they were both exhausted. He also knew that nothing he could say or do would stop or even interrupt them. Their fighting had for them become an end in itself, a release of emotions that paid off like a mad slot machine. They'd keep pulling each other's levers as long as their voices lasted, neither willing to admit defeat.

What held them together, Jamie realized, was a sequence of serious misjudgements, first to be married at all, and then to stay together when every reason and instinct must have told them to abandon it and flee.

Neither one could bring about an ending, only short truces, neither wanting to admit being vanquished, neither wanting to look foolish in the eyes of relatives and friends. In a perverse way, their clashes cemented their loyalty, and loyalty is a powerful force even where that stubborn allegiance is astoundingly misplaced. The pendulum of their emotional discontent swung from silence to shouting, which neither could bring to any conclusion except resignation. Jamie had long ago recognized that, strangely, he could not conceive of either of them living alone or apart. The raw actuality was that they clutched at each other for mutual support while drowning in a sea of despair. This was their life. They had no other.

Soon it was time for Dick to leave for Prince Albert, just before Labour Day, with Jamie's rail ticket to Montreal calling for his departure four days later. They agreed to meet at the Empire, and then took a case of twelve Old Bohemian to the riverbank in the warm sunshine before Dick set out for his drive north. Each was conscious that they would not meet again for at least a year and both knew that major changes were in store, new beginnings. They sat quietly for a while, floating on private thoughts.

"Sorry I wasn't in town the last time you came down to Regina. I was out of town at Linda's farm with her parents. I think it's working out really well with us. And how are your mom and dad?"

"Awful. Very bad. They depress the hell out of me."

"Don't be depressed, ol' buddy. As you say, there's not a damn thing you can do about it. And you've got London to look forward to."

"Yeah, but I wish they were in better shape, happier. It's not as though I've spent a lot of time with them lately, but a year away is a long time. Still—I dunno—I want to go and it's important to me and I must go, but maybe the timing of it all isn't just perfect."

"Hell, timing is never perfect, and even if it were you'd never be sure of it till long after the event. We never know. We have to go with the flow like our friend the river here. It flows north, and that's where

I'm headed too, and as the man said, 'Even the weariest river winds somewhere safe to sea.'"

"Uh hunh. So now you're going to come on all poetic and philosophical while drifting away and turning your back on Europe, travel, the whole meghilla, as Helen would say. I'll bet you'll find it a bit difficult to be poetic during a winter in Prince Albert. Saskatoon blizzards can be bad enough."

"Or good enough. Real enough. The difference between us is that I know what I want, and I'm not at all sure you do."

"Of course I do," Jamie exclaimed, with more conviction than he truly felt. "I want travel, excitement, challenge, stretching, new horizons."

"Do you see a lot wrong," asked Dick, "with this horizon?"

"No. I'll grant you that. No." Jamie opened two more beers and they contemplated the river in silence for several minutes.

In the glory of the huge azure sky a light frisky breeze played with a few cottony clouds. The sky was as high as prairie hopes, as limitless as wanting. The strong smooth flow of the river was the defining contrast with the endless dome of blue. No matter how familiar, the panorama never ceased to move Jamie with its extravagant perfection.

"I dunno," said Dick, "if you're not satisfied with life and wonder in this place, in this world, how could you ever be satisfied?"

"There's a river in London, too, you know. I'm reliably assured that the Thames will still be flowing several months from now."

"Ooh, sarcasm. That wouldn't be the same, though."

"And that's the point, it wouldn't be the same. Very different. But the return ticket takes care of all that. We can always come back. If I make a go of this Ph.D. caper I think there's a chance they'd let me come back here to teach, and that would be just fine."

"I hope so," said Dick. "I won't be getting married for at least a year, till I get some money in the bank, and I'd need you here to be my best man, okay?"

"Love to."

Dick went on to sing the praises of Linda and recount how much he liked her parents when he visited their farm.

"And that reminds me of a new Tommy Douglas story I heard about the farmer's daughter," Dick said.

"And a travelling salesman? Tommy doesn't do farmer's daughter jokes."

"Seems he did once. It goes like this. The daughter moved to Regina to work and brought a city boy back to the farm to meet her family. Said, now, you must be nice to George and make a good impression because I'm going to marry him. Well, everybody was nice as pie, and the dinner was very good, and after coffee the father took George outside to show him around the farm. Showed him the barn and the cattle and the south forty and the dugout, then took him into the back garden. 'Oh,' said George, 'what wonderful vegetables you grow, Mr. Brown!' 'Nothin' to it,' said Mr. Brown, 'just lots of manure, you know.' 'And what excellent flower beds!' 'Manure is the thing, lots of manure.' 'Your lilac bushes are very impressive.' 'Manure is the secret, Ph.D. – Piled higher and Deeper – just manure.' The daughter rushed to her mother and cried, 'You've *got* to do something about father. He's in the garden with George and all he's talking about is manure, manure! Can't you get him to say *fertilizer*?' 'Mary, I've tried and tried, but it's taken me twenty years to get him to say manure.'"

They both rocked with laughter. "I'm certain Tommy said 'Ph.D.'," Jamie objected, "but it's a good story."

"In this imperfect world," Dick smiled, "sometimes we must embellish just a bit. But look, if I'm to get your old car up to P.A. by nightfall, or even Thanksgiving, I'll have to get going. Should I drive you back into town first?"

"Thanks, no, I think I'll stay here by the river for a while longer, then walk back across the campus."

The lilt of a meadow lark's warble sweetened the silence.

"Well," said Jamie, "so long for now, Farmer Brown, and good luck." They shook hands solemnly.

"Good luck to you, George. Give my regards to Buckingham Palace, and drop me a postcard."

Dick turned and walked to the car. Each wondered if they'd ever be as happy again as they had been in Saskatoon. Neither looked back.

XVI

Jamie was thrilled by London. After finding a place to live, a large flat in Hampstead shared with two American friends of Ellie Jensen, he spent half a day shopping for books on Tottenham Court Road and then walked and walked for the next three days: Westminster, Parliament, Trafalgar Square and the National Gallery, Soho, the Strand, Pall Mall, Chelsea …. One afternoon he and Ellie went down the river by water bus as far as Greenwich, goggling at the bridges and ships and the riverbanks. Samuel Johnson said that 'who is tired of London is tired of life', and Jamie couldn't imagine being tired. In a pub called the Cheshire Cheese off Fleet Street he sat down and wrote postcards to Helen, Dick, Uncle Milt, Norman Ward, and his parents as though his wide-eyed enthusiasm made him the first North American to discover England.

Almost every day brought him excitement. For a lad just off the prairie, everything was new and different and to be marveled at: travelling on the underground trains, riding on the top deck of the buses, the British Museum, Hyde Park, wandering in Bloomsbury and the King's Road, St. Paul's, cheap last-minute theatre seats for matinées in the West End, the quality of the serious newspapers and the B.B.C. London seemed to him infinitely wonderful, not least Ronnie Scott's Jazz Club in Soho and Raymond's Review Bar where he goggled at the strippers, beautiful women taking off their clothes to slow, sensuous music, a luxury not afforded him in Saskatoon.

Ellie proved a real treat and soon a close friend. She was petite with a rich cascade of long blonde hair, big luminous brown eyes, small pert breasts, and a great sense of humour. Bright and quick, she frequently advised him on English manners and mores, where to buy necessities inexpensively, and some of the best places to eat cheaply.

He was amused and surprised by how snooty and condescending English men were to any foreigner, any non-plummy accent. English males all appeared to brandish umbrellas like weapons and walk as though they had a bean up their ass. Scotsmen, Welshmen, and the Irish were as open and cordial as Americans, but Englishmen would respond to any request for directions or any conversational overture in a pub with a withering stare as though you'd violated their privacy if not their sister. Young English women, on the other hand, were as delightfully friendly as wet puppies. Compared to girls in Saskatoon, they were remarkably sophisticated in their knowledge of birth control and more than willing to put their information to the frolicsome test. This added considerably to his happy experience and his confidence.

Jamie was also impressed by the range and depth of knowledge available at the London School of Economics, not only among the faculty, but also among the students who most certainly ranked among the best and brightest products of all universities in the English-speaking world. It gradually dawned on him, happily, that his own academic preparation for graduate studies had been very sound and that his professors in Saskatchewan had also been first rate by any scale, better than he had realized until he began to make conscious comparisons. Why is it that we seldom understand what was best in our surroundings until we leave them?

Another enlightening surprise was Paris. Both Jamie's two American roommates had more money than he, and more varied experience. Brad was from New York and prided himself on his worldly *savoir faire* and mixing a killer martini; David's parents were both physicians in Ohio, very affluent, and his generous allowance fattened his scholarship enough that he could buy a used car, a Rover, and could tootle the three of them around the English countryside. Together they drove on weekends to

Bath and Stonehenge and Canterbury and Oxford, sometimes taking Ellie with them, but the highlight of the boys' travels was by road and ferry to Paris for four days in November.

Jamie found Paris exhilarating. London has character, Paris has charm. London is solid, Paris light and beautiful. The complacent elegance of London contrasts with the Parisian insouciant style. The flirty skirts and pert bottoms of girls on the Boule' Miche' overmatched the staid London derrières. Regina was never like this.

The French capital so entranced Jamie that he later decided to spend Christmas there. David and Brad went home for the holidays by airplane, still a very big thing in 1955, but Ellie agreed to accompany him. They could afford only three nights in a tiny hotel on Rue Jacob, but wandered through the city for hours and hours on the Left Bank and Montmartre, usually settling in to a sidewalk café on the Boulevarde St. Germain, Les Deux Magots, or at Le Select in Montparnasse. They drank a lot of coffee and cheap wine, and Jamie learned to stretch a glass of Pernod for an hour. Christmas dinner was turkey sandwiches at Le Dome and better, he thought, than his mother's cooking. Snuggling and sporting in a narrow Parisian bed with the delectable Ellie seemed to him the best Christmas present he'd ever had. If only Roy could see him now.

After a round of parties at New Year's, Jamie and even his two American roommates settled down to a serious stint of work. Professor Abel-Smith had given him a lot of guidance and a lengthy up-to-date bibliography of comparative international publications on healthcare delivery systems and he was determined to master it. Long hours in the school library proved rewarding, although there was relatively little reliable data on Canada. Jamie began to sketch the outline and bones for a thesis with the tentative title, *British and French Experience with Public Health Insurance: Lessons for Canada*, and the more he worked on it the more promising it seemed. Progress was slowed, however, by the urgent temptations of London and by his unfamiliarity with French which he could puzzle out only haltingly with a dictionary and guesses at the translation of many technical terms. Letters to and from his parents faltered a bit because he was so caught up in his subject which he knew would not interest his mother and would exasperate his father.

One day toward the end of February a little blue aerogramme form appeared in his mailbox. Canadian stamp. Vaguely familiar handwriting but not instantly recognized. Hell's bells. It was from his father, the first letter he'd ever received from him. My god, please don't let it be bad news, don't let anything be wrong. Carefully he slit it open.

> *Dear Jamie,*
>
> *I guess the only way to tell you this is straight out. Your mother died last week. Those moles on the side of her neck were melanoma, cancerous, and all of a sudden spread rapidly. I'm sorry about it.*
>
> *Didn't see much point in phoning you. Boats too slow and planes far too expensive for you to come. Nothing to be done anyhow. Your sainted Uncle Milt was out of town at the time and I didn't know where to find him, so he wasn't there either. It was just a small service.*
>
> *Hope your work is going well.*
>
> *Very sorry,*
>
> *Regards,*
>
> *Dad*

Jamie sat down, in shock, devastated. He wrung his hands. He wept. Stood up and paced the room, sat down again and stared at the wall. More sobbing and tears overcame him. First Roy, and now this. He was not in control of himself and walked up High Street to Hampstead Heath, past the big pub on the hill, Jack Straw's Castle, and out on the greensward where he found a bench and sat down. Re-reading his father's curt letter over and over, trying to squeeze more information out of it, didn't help. He blamed himself for being in England, for not being there. The letter didn't make any sense to him, simply declaring the unthinkable, and yet he could not argue with any sentence in it or think of anything he might have done. Without a big bank balance or a magic carpet there was no possible way he could have flown home in time to … to do what? To do nothing. To witness the end of what he had always known, his mother's unhappy and truncated life. Maybe death was her only release, her only remedy.

For the next several nights his fitful sleep was disturbed by two recurring dreams. In one he sat opposite his mother, she seated on her favourite small needlepoint chair with her hands folded, he opening and closing his mouth but unable to emit any sounds or words, incapable of telling her what he felt. Silence can be worse than not knowing what to say. The other dream was of falling through space, arms and legs flailing helplessly as he tumbled through thin air toward a choppy sea in which he knew he would surely drown. Sometimes he knew he would deserve to drown. Other times he hoped against hope that he could learn to float. Sometimes he sank into the waves and awoke with gasping panic. Other times his mother's arms reached out and saved him. No matter which dream seized him, he always woke wondering why the life of so good a woman could have been so cruelly wasted. Having survived so many years of hopeless austerity and deprivation, why could she not have been granted at least enough time to see her own house with her own fireplace, or even to travel, to fulfill some of her lifelong hopes? Everything about her experience seemed unjustly incomplete and now it was ended, a life of such stoicism that he could not comprehend it. Death, always a mystery, also seemed to him iniquitous, wrong, absurd. Still, the ultimate paradox to confront is meaninglessness. In the face of a mute God we search for purpose, need purpose, and finding none know only despair. Someone much wiser than he had said, it is because we fail to understand life that we cannot understand death.

A cloud of guilt and gloom pursued him for several weeks, undermining his work and his pleasure. He did not write back to his father to acknowledge his letter. When his cheerful roommates proposed another visit to Paris at Easter he begged off, citing lack of time and money, but really because of a disinclination to indulge himself. Even London seemed less appealing; he'd lost a bit of his psychological edge. Ellie found him less lively. Work seemed his only refuge.

At the beginning of May Jamie was roused out of his torpor by the pressing realization that he would soon have to leave England. This quickened the pace of his weekend travelling. He and Ellie went by rail to Cambridge, Edinburgh, and Exeter. For one extended weekend they shared the cost of a rented car and toured the Cotswolds, bopping around from village to village, splurging on some lovely country inns. His vitality and zest for living returned. He felt passionately that Britain was a place he would always want to come back to, and that the year had been one of the great formative experiences of his life. It had been a grand adventure.

Before leaving London he had to face leaving Ellie. The prospect jolted him. He couldn't imagine being without her. Belatedly, with a surge of emotion like a tsunami, he knew that he was in love with her. Close friendship with a girl, once taken for granted, can sneak up on you and turn into a huge surprise, grab at the heart and flash into something entirely different. It wasn't just her insouciant laugh or her svelte body or her nimble mind, but that they complemented and fitted each other so absolutely and agreed on almost everything. Except marriage.

Once he'd decided to propose, he took her to the San Lorenzo, their favourite restaurant, near Covent Garden. It served Veal Garibaldi, rolled veal stuffed with mozzarella cheese in a sauce of pineapple and Grand Marnier. Ellie always loved that, with a red Barolo Chianti. When he thought he had her softened up and receptive he popped the question.

She was silent for a moment and looked at him solemnly. "You're not joking, Jamie, you're serious."

"Of *course* I'm serious. I love you and I want you to marry me. Will you? Say you will."

"Wow. I'm surprised. Flattered, touched, just very surprised. I never expected this. I mean, you're 22 and I'm 24, and we've known each other for almost a year, but it isn't something we've ever talked about before. And it isn't as though you have a good job or a pile of money in the bank to support a wife. Aren't you going back to Canada at the end of June?"

"Yes, does that matter?"

"Of course it does. I have a job here that I really like, once only dreamed of, and I have prospects. I haven't even thought of leaving my chance on Fleet Street without giving it a full good run. So I'm much less keen to return to Canada for a few years, at least, maybe ever ...." She let that sentence trail off.

"I could get a job here, easily. I could find a good position in health research, or I guess I could teach school, maybe in a good private school. Staying here and making a good salary shouldn't be a problem."

"And give up on your Ph.D.? Give up on a career as a professor? We both know that's what you want. I couldn't ask you to do that."

"I would, I'd do it, if that's what you want."

"No, please, no. I think you're wonderful, Jamie, a terrific guy, enthusiastic and bright and kind and funny, all the good things, but no. Thanks for asking. It gives me a big lift, really. Maybe I'm the one who's got it wrong. We've had some great times, great trips, a happy and memorable year, and I'm truly grateful, but it will have to end as I—as we both— assumed it would with you sailing back to the west and me staying here. With the fondest of memories, but ...."

They lingered over cups of espresso, then walked hand in hand along the Strand and down to the Embankment to watch the boats glide by on the river before taking the tube back to her flat to make love quietly, but it was not the same. They both knew that the sands had shifted and their time had run out.

Bittersweet is a taste hard for the young to savour. Each of them nursed regrets, but secretly he was relieved. He knew she was right. Somehow her steady and warm good sense made their parting easier.

In early July he returned to Canada and to Saskatoon to be Dick's best man. Linda and Dick chose to have only a small wedding rather than a big formal thrash. Only immediate family and a handful of friends were invited; it was a warm and intimate event. Helen Rivkin pleaded pressure of work and could not attend, but Milt came up for the ceremony and visited, dispensing gifts and good cheer. After the newly weds disappeared, hurrying north for a honeymoon at Lake Waskesiu, Milt urged that they drive south together for a few days, but Jamie could not bring himself yet to return to Regina.

To this refusal Milt only nodded. It pleased him that Jamie seemed more mature, more determined. They parted with the promise that Milt would visit him in Toronto.

XVII

The following two years were a time of re-grouping and consolidation. Helen flourished as a journalist in Vancouver, adding a Saturday opinion column to her regular political reporting. Dick became a popular teacher of English and history in his high school and was elected an alderman in Prince Albert on his first run. He and Linda had a son they named James Douglas Slater after Jamie and Tommy.

Jamie found the University of Toronto more than satisfying. He was given a place in the University College men's residence as a Don, a supervisor of a house of undergrads, which provided him with a small but comfortable flat on campus, and the free room and board enabled him to live very well on his Canada Council scholarship.

He spent one academic year taking four Ph.D. seminars, three in economics, and one in history with the great conservative scholar Donald Creighton on Sir John A. Macdonald which reminded him that the left-wing view of politics was not the only tenable one. Economic theory gave him some trouble and cost him extra time, but economic history and a course in public policy formulation were both breezes. His second year at the U of T was spent doing some work in his thesis and reading widely for the general Ph.D. comprehensive exams, which he passed in the spring.

One of his few regrets was that Harold Innis, an intellectual hero of his, died before Jamie arrived in Toronto. Innis was *the* great economic historian of Canada and, in the latter part of his career, a pioneer in the study of communications and media who prepared the way for Marshall

McLuhan's crucial breakthroughs. A demanding scholar and Dean of the U of T graduate school from 1947 to 1952, it was Innis who set the daunting classic question on a doctoral comprehensive exam which sent laughter and shivers through Ph.D. candidates: "You have three hours. Discuss the economic and political implications of water." One student was said to have quit on the spot and gone off to sell used cars.

With Innis gone, Jamie came under the influence of the distinguished Hungarian scholar Karl Polanyi who, with Innis, was one of the two greatest economic historians of the century. Amazingly, Polanyi lived in Pickering, Ontario. Innis, prejudiced against "wogs", declined to hire him, and Mrs. Illona Polanyi was barred from the United Stated as a Red during the McCarthy period because of certain political activities in Budapest as a girl in 1919, so Karl commuted by train once every two weeks to New York to teach in the graduate school at Columbia. This underlined for Jamie a striking characteristic of Toronto's old WASP society – its deep prejudice against Catholics, Jews, blacks, French Canadians and non-Anglo-Saxon immigrants, a trait he found puzzling and deplorable.

At the beginning of term in 1958 Jamie took a new friend to lunch at his college's High Table where he had privileges as a Don. They found themselves seated across from Professor Donald Creighton and the doyen of English studies, A. S. P. Woodehouse. Jamie made the introductions. "This is Professor Peter Dembowski, a newcomer to the French Department." Silence, no nods. "He's a specialist in medieval French, just arrived from Harvard." Silence, no acknowledgements. Jamie began to burble. "Peter was a young fighter in the Warsaw uprising. He put himself through university here by working at railroad construction, um, with the C.P.R., in the north, and he ...." Ignoring him, Woodehouse spoke. "Isn't it odd, Donald, how one now meets, even at one's own High Table, persons whose names end in 'ski', or 'chuk'?" Jamie and Dembowski of course got up quickly and left. For a city with pretensions to being "world class", and in a university that harboured giants like Northrop Frye, Innis, McLuhan, and C.B. MacPherson, it was astonishing to encounter among the puritan old guard views so narrow and parochial as to make Saskatoon seem positively cosmopolitan.

And in some ways, particularly in the field of social policy, Saskatchewan was becoming the leader in North America. In April 1959 Premier Douglas announced that his government was preparing to introduce medicare legislation by the following year. He reaffirmed the government's intentions in a radio broadcast in December. "If we can do this—and I feel sure we can—then I would like to hazard the prophecy that before 1970 almost every other province in Canada will have followed the lead of Saskatchewan. Once more Saskatchewan has the opportunity to lead the way. Let us therefore have the vision and courage to take this step, believing that it is another advance toward a more just and humane society." He promised to appoint a broadly representative committee, including physicians, to advise the cabinet as to what type of medicare plan would best suit the province. Dr. Walter P. Thompson, a distinguished scientist recently retired as president of the University of Saskatchewan, would be chairman of the committee.

The Premier made it clear that no matter what scheme was chosen or what method of paying doctors arrived at—whether by fee-for-service or capitation or salary—the plan should conform to five basic principles:

- Medical bills would be pre-paid, a public single-payer system. Patients would not be billed.

- The plan must be universal, covering every citizen regardless of age or physical disability.

- High quality of service. Medicare costs should not compromise spending on other existing health services.

- The plan was not to subsidize private insurance companies, but to operate under public control, administered by an independent Commission responsible to the legislature.

- Medicare legislation must be acceptable to both patients and doctors before it was implemented.

The public response of the provincial College of Physicians and Surgeons was of course to warn of trouble ahead and to accuse the government of intending to regiment doctors as civil servants paid by salary. The government replied that it had no such intention and would be guided by the decisions of the Thompson advisory committee.

That committee included nominees from business, labour, the university, government, and the College of Physicians. Appointed in April 1960 and charged with reporting by December, the advisory body found it could make little headway because the doctors' representatives used every possible opportunity and tactic to delay if not block the report. The doctors insisted that there should be no time limit on the deliberations.

The CCF government, recognizing that the doctors were attempting to stonewall or hijack any report, decided to make medicare and the five basic principles the centerpiece of its platform in the spring election of 1960. The voters would decide. The Premier was confronted by a physician on a Regina television forum in March and asked how he could pretend that the Medical Care Advisory Committee was studying the issues when the government had already made up its mind. Douglas replied that the answer to that was simple. If people did not want a program of complete public medical insurance they should vote against the government. "The people of this province will decide whether or not they want a medical care program. The advisory committee will determine the terms and conditions, the schedule of fees, and so on."

The election campaign was a tough one and sometimes got ugly. Everyone knew that if the CCF won, some form of medicare would result. Having first been elected in 1944, it was clear that a victory for the government in 1960 and another term in office would mean that the socialists would have been in power for an unbroken period of twenty years. To many of the CCF's opponents it seemed to be a case of do or die, now or never, and the Liberals under Ross Thatcher pulled out all the stops. The doctors also spent lavishly in the campaign to oust the government.

Once the doctors realized that they could not out-manoeuvre or delay the report of the Advisory Committee indefinitely, and that Douglas was prepared to stand or fall on the medicare issue, they began to gear up for vigourous action. They raised almost $100,000 to finance a campaign to swing public opinion, $60,000 from individual physicians and $35,000 from the Canadian Medical Association, more than any of the provincial political parties could afford to spend. A circular from the president of the College of Physicians to all doctors informed them that a three-man committee with headquarters at 2127 Albert Street, Regina would "… gather and disseminate important data on medical economics to both the profession and the public …. We have obtained the loan of a professional public relations officer …. It is strongly suggested that for purposes of unity and clarity of thought every doctor contact the Special Committee office … prior to making statements on policy or medical economic matters. If possible, doctors are urged to send copies of what they said to this office."

It was lucky for the government that many of the doctors' statements in the campaign were so extreme and intemperate as to stretch public credulity and rebound against the College of Physicians, even with the Liberal opposition party's tacit endorsement. The College had apparently studied the tactics of the American Medical Association in opposing similar initiatives in the United States. The public was bombarded by an extraordinary deluge of media statements on television and radio, full page ads in newspapers, the appearance of a new newspaper called *The Weekly Mirror*, prepared by the College's public relations staff, and direct mailings. Every household in Saskatchewan received a folder in which a leading doctor described practitioners who would be imported to replace M.D.s who fled the province: "They'll have to fill up the profession with the garbage of Europe. Some European doctors who come out here are so bad we wonder if they have ever practiced medicine."

The government's approach, said a College publicity kit, "... is just the same as it was when first enunciated by Karl Marx in his Communistic Theories ...." Another thrust of the College was to warn and frighten Catholic women: "A government controlled plan offers a latent but potential threat to certain dogmas and views of the Catholic Church relating to maternity, birth control and the state ...." Government bureaucrats might consign women with menopausal problems to psychiatric clinics or insane asylums.

Democracy presupposes and requires rationality, a quality which was stretched and distorted during the election campaign. Reasonable arguments can be met and debated, evidence and facts can be weighed pro and con, but the prevalent use of lies and scare tactics was hard to offset. Patiently and with restraint government spokesmen and Premier Douglas tried to put their case. The privacy of patients and their health records would not be violated. Salaries for doctors were not being considered. There would be total freedom for doctors to reject patients and for patients to choose doctors. The independent professional status of medical practitioners would not be changed in any way; only the method of payment was to be altered. Medicare would be administered by an independent public commission much as the previous Hospital Insurance Plan had been worked out, and which had proven so efficient and popular as to be copied in all other provinces. Most important, families and individuals who could not afford costly private insurance, which often refused payment for certain procedures and "pre-existing conditions", would be able to receive treatment regardless of their ability to pay and not be bankrupted.

These were essentially sensible if defensive arguments, but in the highly charged emotional environment of the campaign it was difficult to get the message out in the face of hostile advertising by doctors and Liberal attacks in the privately owned media. The outcome of the election was by no means certain.

During the bitter campaign, Tommy Douglas gave a long and revealing interview to a reporter from the Toronto *Star Weekly*.

When I was a boy in Scotland before World War I, I fell and hurt my knee. A bone disease called osteomyelitis set in and for three or more years I was in and out of hospital.

My father was an iron moulder and we had no money for doctors, let alone specialists.

After we immigrated to Canada the pain in my knee came back. Mother took me to the out-door clinic of a Winnipeg hospital.

They put me in the public ward as a charity patient and I still remember the young house doctor saying that my leg must be cut off.

But I was lucky. A brilliant orthopaedic surgeon, whose name was Smith, came through the wards looking for patients he could use in teaching demonstrations. He examined my swollen knee and then went to see my parents. 'If you'll let me use your boy to help teach medical students,' he said, 'I think I can save his leg. His knee may never be strong again but it can be saved.'

I shall always be grateful to the medical profession for the skill that kept me from becoming a cripple, but the experience of being a charity patient remains with me.

Had I been a rich man's son the services of the finest surgeons would have been available. As an iron moulder's boy, I almost had my leg amputated before chance intervened and a specialist cured me without thought of a fee.

All my adult life I have dreamed of the day when an experience like mine would be impossible and we would have in Canada a program of complete medical care without a price tag. And that is what we aim to achieve in Saskatchewan by 1961, the finest health service available to everyone in the province, regardless of ability to pay. This is our goal of a compulsory prepaid medical care insurance.

To Jamie and to many others that was the most sane and humane statement made by any politician during the 1960 campaign. It may rank as one of the best, simple utterances in our political history.

It was only after most of the provincial campaign was over that Jamie arrived in Regina. He had not been able to leave Toronto until late May, traveling by car, a 1956 Chev he'd recently purchased on term payments, and reached Saskatchewan June 3rd. A letter had been sent ahead to his father saying he'd like to stay with him for a week, but there was no reply. On arrival he found the back door of the house unlocked, a bed made up for him, and a note from his father on the kitchen table saying he hoped that his son had not come back just to vote for those S.O.B. socialists and that Commie premier. "So far we've avoided bloodshed and I'm certain we can get out the votes to defeat the CCF anti-doctor bastards, but it will be close. See you at supper. I may be late. Dad."

Jamie phoned around to several friends and to Helen's dad, Dr. Rivkin, to get a better idea of the political landscape, and also read some material in a kit circulated by the College of Physicians which had been left prominently on the kitchen counter. He was amazed at the virulence of the anti-medicare propaganda and the personal attacks on Premier Douglas. It all seemed to him very sad, and violated all of his understandings of political fair play.

Over a late supper of hamburgers seared on the barbecue his father crowed that he worked most evenings and every weekend campaigning for the Liberals. He cursed the government at great volume and length, but Jamie didn't respond.

"Did you read the material by the docs I left on the counter?"

Jamie nodded.

"It's good stuff, don't you think?"

"Highly unusual, very interesting."

"Well. Is that all you can say? I suppose you'd rather talk about your mother?"

"No. I wouldn't. Not right now."

"Okay. So I guess you came home at this point in hopes of casting a ballot, did you, with some fake ID saying that you live here?"

"My ID isn't fake. Actually I've always kept my Saskatchewan driver's licence, renewed by mail every year, so that I could qualify for provincial auto insurance since it's the cheapest in Canada."

"Humph! And using what address, should I ask?"

"This address, your house. All perfectly legal and above board."

"Good. That makes it easier for me to alert every polling station in the area that you can't vote, that your address is phony, that you've lived in Toronto these past years, and before that you were out of the country gallivanting around and getting indoctrinated in the Soviet Union or some other damn fool place. Damned if I'll have my vote cancelled out by a bolshevik in the family. How do you like that?"

"Whatever you say, Dad."

"I do say. And have you seen your blessed Uncle Milt yet? No? Just as well. The bastard does business around here but I know for a fact that he hasn't contributed one thin dime to the Liberal party. Might even be crazy enough to vote for the government, I suspect."

Jamie bit his lip and remained silent. Obviously this warm and cozy family conversation was going nowhere. His dad allowed as how he wouldn't be around much till after the election but that it would be all right if his pinko son stayed a few days, and went off to bed. Jamie wished, as so very often he wished, that Roy was there, not only for companionship but to steady him in his efforts not to assault his father.

Volunteering to do door-to-door canvassing and stuff envelopes for the CCF kept Jamie busy in the daytime, and in the evenings he had dinner twice with Milt in the restaurant of the Bluebird Motor Inn and Lounge, once with Helen's parents in their home, all very enjoyable. Dr. Abe Rivkin's optimism was guarded, but he thought that Tommy would pull through. "Lord," he said, "I hope so."

Tempers and tensions were high on election day, June 8th. Voter turnout was heavy and a lot of fingernails were bitten to the quick late in the day before last returns trickled in from rural areas and the north. People on both sides of the issue held their breath on into the evening until it became clear that the government had been returned to power with an increased majority in the legislature. The CCF won thirty-eight of fifty-four seats. Jamie joined thousands of others dancing in the streets of downtown Regina and cheered himself hoarse, then drove by the Rivkin's house and, seeing all their lights on, went in and drank a glass of champagne with them and a festive group of their friends.

The other drinking in the family was done by his father. Lorne McRae fell into a fit of anger and despondency and stayed drunk for four days.

The future of medicare was now secure, or so Jamie believed. Tommy had his mandate. But is anything in this fragile world safe or secure?

XVIII

After the election Jamie drove up to Saskatoon to see Norman Ward. He also dropped in on several others of his favourite professors and strolled the lush campus and the riverbank. Then he headed north to visit Dick and Linda in Prince Albert. Weeks earlier he had written to them saying that he'd be driving from Toronto to Regina, and Dick had replied that he'd meet him halfway. That turned out to mean not Kenora or even Winnipeg but halfway up from Regina, at Saskatoon. Whatever.

The three of them took side trips to Batoche and Fort Carlton and to Candle Lake where the Slaters were dickering to buy a cottage. Linda proved a good cook and bright and a sweetie; Jamie liked her a lot. Evenings they sat and drank rye and argued and talked into the wee small morning hours even though Dick had to be on deck to teach in the morning. They talked about everything: god, life, love and destiny, but mostly about politics and the recent provincial election. They raised glasses to toast the government's victory.

"Tommy was lucky, though," Dick said, "that Ottawa and the feds came through with a commitment to pay fifty per cent of the costs of the provincial Hospital Insurance schemes. That gave our man enough money to tackle medicare. Otherwise it would have been pretty damn difficult to swing."

"Oh, I don't know. I thought that was inevitable. I mean, once our Hospital plan proved so popular and every other province in the country copied it, the pressure on the feds to kick in half was pretty heavy. There's nothing more clamourous than the provincial Treasurers showing up in Ottawa with their hands out. But if the feds had been the least bit serious about either Hospital Insurance or medicare they could have created them from the center decades ago and not waited to be pushed by Saskatchewan. And pushed they bloody well will be when our medicare is up and running. The other provinces will jump on the bandwagon, you just watch."

"Probably, but it's not all in place yet."

"It will be, and by early next year, 1961, never fear," Jamie said.

"I suppose, but …."

"Hey, did you manage to find that quote from Tommy in the legislature in April 1954 that I asked you about in my letter? From way back when we used to run across Waskana Lake to the House to hear him? I want it for something I'm writing."

"I did, yes. Had it somewhere in an old box of notes, and buried, but I found it again in the public library. Here it is:

> *I made a pledge with myself long before I ever sat in this House, in the years when I knew something about what it meant to get health services when you don't have the money to pay for it. I made a pledge with myself that some day if I ever had anything to do with it, people would be able to get health services just as they are able to get educational services, as an inalienable right of being citizens of a Christian country.*

Good stuff eh? We didn't know then how privileged we were to hear him say it. And he never let us down."

"Right," said Jamie. "Absolutely. Now, with a comfortable majority of sixteen seats in the house, he's home and dry."

"You're so naïve, ol' buddy, so painfully naïve and credulous. I think the battle has just begun. There'll be hell to pay yet, I'm afraid."

"What? Why? The government introduces a medicare bill to the legislature, it passes, and Bob's your uncle. I don't see any problem."

"You don't. All right, let me put another scenario to you. First, the Medical Care Advisory Committee gets hung up, well into next year, because the medical reps won't agree to anything. Second, the Liberal opposition tries to obstruct with a loud hue and cry about the government having only a plurality of the popular vote in that election, not a majority."

"But thirty-eight of fifty-four seats? You can't argue with that."

"Ross Thatcher and the opposition can, and will. You're the big deal intellectual, you do the math: Liberals 33 per cent of the popular vote, Conservatives 14 per cent, Social Credit 12 per cent, leaving the CCF at 41 per cent. The opposition will say, not enough. Oh, I know, that's an entirely normal split under our voting system, where majority governments seldom get fifty per cent of the vote. Still, the opposition will say, not enough."

"But the Liberals said they favoured *some* form of medicare."

"Some form, mainly private insurance, but not the CCF form. So, third, the Liberals demand a plebiscite, delaying things another, what, six months? twelve months?"

"I can't believe you're saying this. I suppose it's possible, but surely …."

"Wait. The fourth line of attack, a humdinger, would be the doctors digging in their heels and refusing to co-operate, refusing to participate."

"You can't be serious."

"I am. Entirely serious. A doctor's strike."

"That's … that's just too awful to contemplate."

"Face it, Mr. Theorist, in practice it could work. A lot of things point that way, I think. Having lost an election, being led by a small group of ideologues and some specialist docs who are refugees from the British National Health Service which is short of money, they might panic. But they're able to raise plenty of funds here for political action and, most important, believing their backs are now against the wall, could go on strike. Maybe cause the government to back down.

Extreme, but a strike could work. No, it's not over, and as they say in show biz, it ain't over till it's over."

The three of them fell silent. Jamie realized that Dick could be right.

"Another drink, boys?" Linda asked. "I think we all need one."

XIX

Before Jamie was up the next morning, a bit hung over, Dick roused him with a shout that Milt was on the phone.

"Huh? Hello?"

"I'm glad I found you there. We've got to talk. Are you awake and tracking?"

"Yup. Sort of. Is something wrong?"

"I'm in Saskatoon again, got here last night. I'm at the hotel, the Bessborough. Can you drive down here and meet me this morning?"

"What's wrong? Sure I can. I will, but is it something about my dad?"

"No, it's not that. I'd really rather not talk about it on the phone. How soon can you get here? By 11?

"By 10, if you say so. I'll just grab a coffee and head out, get there before 10. But I wish you'd say what's up."

"Ten will be soon enough. Just hustle. I'm in room 711." Milt hung up.

It's Roy, Jamie thought, his heart beating fast. It's something about Roy, I just know it. But what? What?

He stuffed his pajamas and travelling gear into a suitcase, accepted a black coffee from Linda, said his goodbyes, and hit the road. Feeling grim and apprehensive, he hammered the throttle and arrived by 9:30. Milt met him in the hotel lobby.

"Let's go in to the coffee shop. Have you had breakfast? No?"

Jamie ordered scrambled eggs on toast and waited for his uncle to open up. "It's about Roy," Milt said.

"I thought it was. I'm ready for it. He's dead, isn't he?"

Milt nodded into his coffee. "It'll take me a couple of minutes to get this out. My news is bad. Lousy. But I wanted you to hear it from me first, not from somebody else, not from the police."

"The police? Why them?"

"An officer from Saskatoon phoned my office yesterday. With your parents, I'd been included on their records as next of kin, because … I'd talked with them about Roy before. They couldn't reach your father, and of course is … so they asked if I'd come up and make an identification. Naturally I drove up as fast as I could." He pushed his coffee aside.

"What had happened was, a fisherman snagged something unusual in the river and talked to a cop about it. A jacket. Well, part of one, without the sleeves. It's a Huskies jacket from the U. of S. hockey team that Roy played for. Badly deteriorated from years in the water, but with some marks in it on the inside collar label, faint, but in indelible ink. The police thought they were initials, R.N. or maybe R.M. They checked with the university sports admin people, who took a while to check their files, and the only member of recent varsity teams not known to be alive and accounted for on their lists was, predictably, Roy."

He paused. Jamie's eyes blurred, his gut seized. Although he'd been expecting and imagining something like this for a long time, and certainly since Milt's call to Prince Albert this morning, he still felt as if he'd been kicked in the solar plexus.

"That's not—that's not proof, that's not certainty," he stammered.

"I'm afraid it is." Milt shook his head. "There's more. The inside pocket of the jacket contained a wallet. Contents waterlogged impossibly, of course, unreadable, but the same Moroccan brown leather wallet, unmistakably the kind I gave each of you one Christmas all those years ago. There can't be any doubt, Jamie. I wish there could be, but there isn't."

Jamie fumbled and pulled his own well-worn wallet, stared at it as though he'd never seen it before and wishing that perhaps he hadn't.

"That's the one," said Milt, reaching for it. "Identical. I'm most terribly sorry. I saw Roy's, last night, but if it would give you more certainty we can go down to the police station so you could see for yourself."

"No. Not necessary, no. And I don't want to see it. If you say there isn't any doubt, no."

They sat without speaking for several minutes.

A waitress came by and asked if there'd be anything else. They waved her away.

"But I guess that's the question, isn't it? I mean, will there be anything else? What do we do now? We'll have to run an obituary in the papers after we tell my dad."

"Oh, I should have said that, but I just didn't know where to start. I lost sight of that. I've already told Lorne, about 8:30 this morning when he finally picked up his phone, shortly after I called you."

"And what did he say?"

"I have to tell you it was a pretty bizarre conversation. Me fumbling around not sure how to say it, him either half asleep or half drunk or maybe both. He said the police had already sent him a telegram and he didn't want to hear anything more from them or from me either."

"Sounds like him."

"Yeh, we've never gotten along just perfectly. Anyway, I tried to tell him as best I could and he just got angry and cursed me and ranted. When I kept asking whether I should make any, um, arrangements here he shouted that there was no body so there'd be no funeral and it must all be a case of mistaken identity anyway. I was to stop, he said, just bloody well stop meddling, stop trying to interfere with his family. Anger and denial, that's all I got from him, plus the usual abuse for merely trying to ...."

"I understand. Take it easy, uncle Milt. I get the drift of it clearly enough. I'm sorry. I apologize for him. He's a desperately sad man. I'm sorry for him, too. What a screwed up family, eh? Don't we take the cake? Jeez."

"But you're okay, Jamie. You can handle all this, I'm sure, awful as it is. You're okay?"

"I can live with it. Yes."

Another silence.

"But you know, Milt, for years, every time we've mentioned Roy's disappearance … I assume suicide …?" Milt nodded. "Every time we've mentioned Roy over the years, I've had this twinge, a feeling that you knew more than you wanted to say or could say about it all. Is that true?"

"I'm afraid it is, yes."

"You can tell me more now, can't you? It might help. He must have had a reason, some terrible reason, for what he did. If you know, or even have any idea, please tell me. Now."

Milt nodded again and bit his lips before replying.

"I suppose this is as good or bad a time as any to give you the whole story. Right. But let's get out of here and take a walk, or go out into the park and sit on a bench. That might make it easier."

When they were out in the fresh air by the river and settled on a park bench, Jamie lit a cigarette. Milt unwrapped a long panatella and chewed the end of it morosely. Jamie broke the silence.

"I've believed for a very long time that he was dead or else he'd have been in touch with me. So nothing you can say will surprise me. Or change anything."

"Well, it might surprise you a little." He cleared his throat a couple of times, fidgetted, lit his cigar. His story came out slowly and haltingly.

"I've known what happened right from the beginning, but Roy asked me not to say anything, mostly for Jean's sake, and I've kept that promise till now. I'll admit there were a couple of times when I tried to get through to Lorne, raised the subject to give him *some* indication of the circumstances, but he just didn't want to know, wouldn't talk about it, told me to shut the hell up. The 'meddling' issue again, a sore spot, and I guess denial then, too."

"Hell, dad seems to have been in denial about a lot of things most of his life. Petulant. But Milt, you're backing in to it. You still haven't told me …."

"Right again. I'm trying, Jamie, but it's not a pretty story." He paused again. "Do you remember, that last letter from Roy arrived at your parents' house on a Thursday? And then you hitch-hiked to Saskatoon to try to talk to him? I'd talked to him already. After making up his mind and mailing the letter he phoned me late that Wednesday night. He just wanted to explain and to say goodbye. We talked. He was totally calm about it, depressed but lucid and determined. I'd say, gallant. Suicide was his answer to the biggest question. Of course I climbed into my car and drove north immediately, collecting two speeding tickets and arriving just before dawn. A friendly cop to whom I explained things drove ahead of me, lights flashing to give me emergency speeding rights the last part of the way. We were too late. He was gone. I woke his roommate and talked to him, but Roy was gone."

"Why? For the love of God, why? He must have told you."

"He did, yes. He'd been diagnosed by the university doctor as having leukemia. Sooner or later leukemia was always fatal then, as you know, mostly still is now. Roy told me that any long series of radiation treatments would be expensive, terribly costly, and that Lorne and the family couldn't begin to afford them. I told him I could and would of course afford them, but he just gave me that dry chuckle and kept repeating that his mind was made up. He'd read a lot about the disease in medical textbooks and didn't like his prospects. The treatments would be long and debilitating, and he said he was depressed enough without such painful futility. Said it would only postpone the inevitable.

"He answered all my questions and arguments only by repeating that he'd decided how to do it. Asked me to say goodbye to everybody, particularly you and Jean. Told me that he'd got two heavy lead weights from barbells in the gym and would belt them around his waist and simply walk into the river, just above the dam. Which he did, I've no doubt." (My favourite spot, Jamie thought with a shudder. The very place. I'll never be able to go there again.) "His body was never found because it's undoubtedly caught in the back-water under the dam. He definitely went into the waters of the South Saskatchewan and never came out, which is why the authorities listed his disappearance only as 'missing'. I thought of asking the police to send divers under the dam to recover his body, but I decided that would be little help to anybody, particularly Jean, and that 'missing' would be a lot better, gentler, word than 'suicide'. Roy didn't want any drama. All he wanted was a quiet disappearance, the least upsetting way out, and he found that."

Milt rubbed his forehead, stubbed out his cigar. "So there it is. That's all I knew, or know. Except that he was a fine young man, and brave." He heaved a sigh. "Life," he muttered. "Who was it said, we are all 'merely dust postponed'? It's so bloody hard, Jamie, to know what's right. Maybe I should have told you earlier, but ...."

Jamie couldn't think of anything to say. He wept, quietly, for many minutes.

Finally he said, "Isn't it awful that he'd let the cost of treatments influence his decision?"

"Yes. That was only part of it, I think, but, yes."

"If only we had medicare insurance then, he might have accepted treatment, might have gone into remission, might still be alive today."

"I'm not sure. Who can tell? Probably. Or lived longer, at least." Milt paused, then rose to his feet.

"Come on, Jamie me lad, let's go in. I have to be back in Regina by this evening. Meetings, damn it. Will you come along? Your dad may need you now."

"Somehow I doubt that. But yes, I'll be there in a day or two, after I, you know, think things through some more. In a way it's good to know the truth, and not to imagine things any worse, but it's still so damned hard to accept. I'll phone when I arrive, Milt."

They shook hands. Then they grasped each other in a strong hug.

"Okay. Good. I'll see you there."

XX

Before he left Saskatoon, Jamie walked the lush campus for many hours, then arranged a talk with the chairman of the Political Economy department, George Britnell, about what chances he might have of returning to teach at the University of Saskatchewan. His hope was that he might come home to a junior academic appointment, but he was told that no door would swing open until he shaped up and completed his Ph.D. thesis. How long had he been in the program at Toronto? Almost four years? Yes, he'd completed more course work and the comprehensive exams and the two other language requirements, but where was that bloody thesis? He was told bluntly to get it on and get it done. And he knew this advice was right.

Dinner in Regina with Milt, at Champs on Scarth Street, cheered him up a little. Milt could always tell jokes, embellish political gossip and help him relax. There were a few topics, however, on which their conversation was more sombre, and they couldn't yet bring themselves to talk further about Roy.

"Any news of my Dad? Is he okay? After the election he said he didn't want to see me around any more, and went on one helluva bender. Maybe that made it more likely he'd reject the news about Roy."

"All I know," said Milt, "is that he's on some sort of medication for high blood pressure. As I said, he cursed me a lot when I phoned. I thought he'd have apoplexy after the election, and he seemed to flush a bit purple any time the subject of medicare or Tommy came up. There's a very hard core, you know, of right-wingers, probably the most reactionary of all the Liberals in Canada, who seem to feel that they have to save the whole country from socialism single-handed and that they're misunderstood by everyone else. It's sort of a martyr complex, I'd say, and it looks like it will drive them to extremes. They're a very intemperate and cranky lot, apparently convinced that Mike Pearson and the Ottawa Liberals have gone soft, leaving our Saskatchewan boys isolated. And if our local politicians feel cornered and desperate, there's no telling what they might get up to."

"But just after the election when Dr. Kelly, the general secretary of the Canadian Medical Association, announced that the CMA accepted the democratic decision of the electorate and would turn their attention to improving any health insurance scheme, didn't that cut any ice? Wasn't that a positive signal?"

"Maybe, but as you saw, the Saskatchewan section of the CMA repudiated Dr. Kelly's words and insisted that they remained 'unalterably opposed' to Tommy's plan."

"Could be just bluster, reflecting their disappointment," Jamie said. "Not necessarily any real threat."

"Let's hope you're right. Let's hope everybody calms down." They both reflected quietly on that for a moment. Then Milt continued. "Now, when you get back to Toronto, will you bear down on your thesis?"

"Yup. I will. It's first priority."

But when Jamie arrived back on the U of T campus he received a note summoning him to meet with the chairman of his department.

"We're short-staffed, McRae," said the chair, "and we have a lot of classes to cover with big enrolments, so I'll need you as a full-time teacher, starting a month from now, in September. I'm sure you'll pitch in and do well."

"But I don't have the Ph.D. yet. My thesis still has three chapters to go before completion and I ...."

"Doesn't matter, for now. Finish up as rapidly as you can. The first year of preparing lectures can be demanding, time-consuming, I know, and we'll take that into account when we consider your record later on. Remember, the thesis should just be an exercise in competence, not a life's work. Harrumph. One of our senior men is taken ill and won't be available till the New Year, so after shuffling assignments I've got you down for two sections of Eco. 100 and that large class we have to lay on for the Engineering School, which is not overly demanding. Much of your lecture material can be repeated with each group, I'm sure."

"Looks to me like that adds up to about 600 or 650 students, quite a number. Will there be one or two teaching assistants for marking? It's grading essays that takes the time."

"Afraid not. Very little money available this year and our few graduate students qualified to be teaching assistants are already committed to senior faculty. Sorry about that."

"Sounds to me like a pretty tough go."

"Oh, I hope not too heavy. And keep in mind that this year's experience could count for you on a tenure track and, who knows?, if this works out as I hope it will you might possibly have a long-term prospect of staying on staff here. Consider it an opportunity. And your starting salary as a Lecturer will be $5,500 for the year. Satisfactory? Anything else? Good day, Mr. McRae, and good luck."

Jamie retreated and brooded and knew he'd need more than luck. He'd need a lot of prep time and some long nights of diligent work.

With letters from Milt and Dick and an occasional scanning of the Saskatchewan papers he kept abreast of developments at home. The Thompson Advisory Committee was having heavy weather and great difficulty preparing a report. The medical members were willing to agree to nothing. Thompson himself was so frustrated that he wanted to resign but was persuaded by Tommy to keep trying. The government asked him for at least an interim report, and this was produced by a majority of the committee in September, 1961, but without the support of the three physician members or the representative of the Chamber of Commerce who filed a minority report. Some took this to be an ominous sign.

Acting on the majority report, Tommy immediately called a special session of the legislature to introduce the Medical Insurance Act. There would be no premiums levied or deterrent fees, with all costs to be paid out of general provincial revenues. The bill passed into law in November, with the Liberal opposition voting for it on Second Reading, "in principle", but against it on Third and final Reading, raising some objections to details. This allowed the Liberals to claim support for any virtues in the Act but also to condemn any shortcomings. Implementation of the Act was set for April 1962.

By the time the bill was passed Tommy had stepped aside as premier. He yielded to the urging of the "new" party and accepted the national leadership of the New Democratic Party on November 1, 1961, content with having achieved his goal of medicare for Saskatchewan. His successor, chosen by the caucus, was Woodrow Lloyd, a former schoolteacher, and a member of the cabinet since 1944 as Minister of Education. Bright and very able, Lloyd was a tall, bald, serious man, a solid administrator and unflappable, strong and contained. He could never match Tommy in the quick cut and thrust of political debate, but who could?

Premier Lloyd appointed a new Minister of Health, William Davies, and set about establishing a Medical Care Insurance Commission to be headed by Don Tansley, a career civil servant who had been director of the Budget Bureau in the Treasury department. Tansley wrote to the College of Physicians, outlining the proposed basis for payment of doctors and requesting a meeting for discussions. He received no reply. Doctors approached by the government to become members of the Commission declined, and several said that the College "would come down on them like a ton of bricks" if they agreed to participate. They feared that even their licences to practice might be withdrawn or their hospital privileges revoked. Tansley and the new minister of health repeatedly wrote to the College requesting meetings to negotiate details of the Act or consider amendments, but were rebuffed. The College would not co-operate in any way. "We regard this Act," wrote College president Dr. H. D. Dalgliesh, "as a form of civil conscription of the profession of medicine and an attempt to put us under the control of government by political and economic pressure."

In March 1962, Premier Lloyd attempted to resume talks with the College, gave the doctors repeated assurances concerning their professional freedom, and announced that implementation of the Act would be delayed from its proposed date in April until July 1, 1962, pending negotiations.

This may well have given the College some reason to believe that the government would back down. It did not. Neither did the physicians.

Impasse.

With the two sides dug in and the Liberals calling for a plebiscite, Dick Slater wrote an "I told you so" letter to Jamie in April. "You'd better plan to come back here for the summer. There's going to be fireworks."

Faced with a huge stack of final exams to mark and the need to spend the summer working on his thesis, Jamie nonetheless wrote an exploratory letter to his father saying he might come home for a month or two, arriving probably in June. A reply was prompt and abrupt.

> *Don't come. There'll be nothing for an outsider like you to do here, and I don't want to have to explain to my friends that I have a Commie relative. Things are getting more and more tense, and it could get dangerous. If, I'd say when, the doctors stand up and withdraw services, I expect a real confrontation and maybe violence to clear the air. The CCF dictatorship will be brought down by right-minded people.*
>
> *If your man Douglas had been a white man instead of the Red that he is, and brought in a decent medical bill with private insurance and a means test, there'd have been no trouble. But trouble is brewing. MDs*

are preparing to pick up and leave the province. Respectable citizens are not talking to anti-doctor crazies, the community and even families are divided, relatives not speaking to each other, choosing up sides like a civil war. One of my neighbours, not talking to his pro-CCF sister any longer, painted her porch light Red last night. We all got a laugh out of that.

So I don't want to see you until this is over and we whip the socialist bastards, which will be soon, believe me.

In haste,

Dad

Jamie read the letter over again with a heavy heart. Only the second letter his father had ever written to him, and not notably cordial. He began to write a careful reply, outlining his position and noting that the government had offered many concessions to the doctors, including the right to practice outside the Act if they wished, but he realized that his father's position was impermeable to argument and tore it up. Instead he wrote to his Uncle Milt, saying he might be coming west, and Milt phoned him immediately to offer him a welcome and bed and board for as long as he wanted to stay.

Jamie reflected that in fact he should not be going, but remaining on Toronto to complete his thesis. Still, the unfolding drama seemed too important not to witness. He finished his marking and gathered his thesis materials to take on the trip. He couldn't help thinking of the famous statement of the British constitutional authority Walter Bagehot: 'Our parliamentary system pre-supposes a people so fundamentally at one that they may safely appear to differ.'

Not bloody likely, he thought, and finished packing his bags.

XXI

In May 1962, notices were posted in the offices of nearly all doctors in Saskatchewan.

TO OUR PATIENTS

THIS OFFICE WILL BE CLOSED AFTER

JULY 1ST, 1962

WE DO NOT INTEND TO CARRY ON PRACTICE

UNDER THE SASKATCHEWAN

MEDICAL CARE INSURANCE ACT

Two copies of that sign were provided to each MD by the public relations office of the College of Physicians, which also sent along copies of a "personal letter which you may wish to send to your patients:"

> *Dear Patient,*
>
> *You are probably aware that the decision of the Government to put their Medical Care Insurance Act into operation on July 1st prevents me and other doctors in the province from continuing to provide medical services to you and to other patients without accepting the terms and conditions of the Act.*
>
> *I cannot, in all conscience, provide services under the Act and thus my office will be closed on July 1st. It will stay closed until the Government will allow me to treat you, as I have in the past, without political interference or control.*
>
> *You will appreciate that I am deeply concerned about taking what*

must seem to you to be a drastic step. Unfortunately, the attitude of Government leaves me with no other choice. In the interval, our District Medical Society is setting up an Emergency Service so that qualified physicians will be available to treat any serious illness.

While I know that this arrangement is not a suitable substitute for the close medical relationship which has existed between us in the past, closing my office is the only way in which I can voice my many objections to this Act. If you disagree with the actions of the Government, you too should state your objections to your Elected Representatives. It is only in this way that Government will be forced to abandon its plan to institute political control of doctors and patients.

I support medical insurance. I am willing to accept an arrangement which is purely insurance and which does not attempt to control your doctor or tell your doctor how to treat you. I hope that it will be possible to resolve this problem soon and that we may be able to continue the relationship which has existed between us in the past.

Dick Slater, like many people, read and re-read this letter from his GP with amazement. Clearly it was a work of sly political art concocted by a public relations man high on ideology and short on facts. What "political control" of doctors? What "political control" of patients? How could the Medical Care Commissioner or the government *possibly* tell your doctor how to treat you? Why would it want to? In the letter absurdity was piled upon absurdity by some inflamed PR hack schooled in innuendo and right-wing ideology. It would be amazing if it were not so dangerous. It was straight fear mongering. Dick mailed off a copy to Jamie in Toronto with a penciled comment: "Unbelievable. Transparent nonsense and despicable."

However, with many people it had the intended effect. It aroused political passions and panic. Although the medicare scheme proposed no change in the doctor–patient relationship except in the method of payment, with the cost to the public treasury and not the individual patient, many citizens were beset by confusion and doubt and dire forebodings. If ill, how would they find a doctor to treat them? How would they get prescriptions refilled? How would they find a doctor for a sick child? Something must be terribly wrong if physicians refused to treat patients in need. It was unthinkable. Somehow, it must be the fault of the government. After all doctors have never lied to us before. Doctors were honourable people. Weren't they?

Lorne McRae broke into a broad grin when he read the letter from the College of Physicians. That will get people's attention, he thought, that will arouse them. To him, the issue was not whether he could find a doctor, because with his connections he was sure he could, but whether the government would falter and topple in the face of such threats or at least withdraw the legislation and admit defeat. If not, there'd be rioting in the streets. The doctors clearly intended to go out on strike. The strike was on for July 1st, without doubt, and it would teach the socialist bastards a lesson. It made him feel happier than he'd felt in months.

For Dick, and for most editorial writers outside the province, the issue was whether any group, including a profession, has the right to flout the law. Would a doctors' strike constitute civil disobedience or simple violation of the law? Legislation passed by a democratic electorate must be carried out and obeyed or the result will be chaos.

The government, for its part, assumed that the medical profession had no more right to ignore a law passed by a democratically elected legislature than any other body of citizens and that the profession, under the decades old Medical Act spelling out its rights and duties, had a legal and moral responsibility not to abandon its patients. Many lawyers, even if they did not speak up, held this view. The solicitor for the Ontario Medical Association, for example, was blunt: "A doctor can't say 'I'm through' when there is no other doctor available. Under law he has a continuing obligation to patients under treatment. If he leaves them he will be considered to have abandoned them and would be liable for damages." This statement was widely quoted in the press across most of Canada, but not in Saskatchewan.

In the prairie province the daily newspapers fanned the flames of hysteria. Front-page stories played up the impending "withdrawal of physicians' services" and carried full-page ads placed by the College arguing its case. There were few if any full page adds placed by the government in reply, prompting widespread rumours that the big daily papers had declined to print paid ads from the Ministry of Health. One editor commented that a free press had no obligation to accept advertising from organizations of which it disapproved.

Among the smaller weekly papers the Indian Head *News*, for example, ran a full-page anti-CCF ad under a bold banner that stated, "You Are Going to Lose Your Doctors". The main text read: "It will be too late when the pain comes in the middle of the night. When the baby starts choking, when the good farm worker is mangled in the power-takeoff, when the car plunges off the road and scatters dusty bodies in the ditch, when the heart attack comes …. If this sounds emotional, or even hysterical—good."

In an attempt to offset the frenzy and get the government's side before the public, Premier Lloyd, always solemn and careful to avoid inflammatory statements, more often resorted to the public broadcasting system. On CBC-TV in early May he outlined the government's position, gave further assurances concerning the freedom of the doctors under medicare, and spelled out the fundamental question:

> *The issue is whether the people of Saskatchewan shall be governed by a democratically elected legislature responsible to the people, or by a small highly organized group. The people of Saskatchewan have been served notice. The notice is that, until we repeal the Medical Care Insurance Act or unless that group is permitted to ignore this Act of a duly constituted government, the people of the province will be punished*

by curtailment of medical services. It is to be hoped that our individual
doctors will think carefully before they allow their health-giving skills to
be used in this way—as instruments of compulsion and coercion.

Increasingly distressed by eastern media reports of the situation, Jamie
set off by car and headed west. He drove through the US from Sarnia up
through Michigan and over the Mackinac Straits, then along the south
shore of Superior to Duluth and to Grand Forks and Minot, ND. His
car radio tuned to PBS kept him informed of the progress of President
J. F. Kennedy's medical bill in Congress, a plan to extend public medical
insurance to the elderly. The American Medical Association vehemently
attacked Kennedy's bill as "a cruel hoax" and warned that the public was
being "blitzed, brain-washed and bandwagoned into swallowing a plan
that would turn individuals into numbers." Not much help there, he
thought. (Later, in July, the US Senate killed the bill by a vote of 52 to
48, another serious setback for public health insurance.)

When he turned north from Minot and reached the border crossing
at North Portal he was startled to see that a slashing of crimson paint
had altered the 'Welcome' sign to read 'Welcome to Red Canada', a
sharp reminder of why he was making the trip. Now he heard frequent
radio announcements on a private station, CKCK Regina, that the
government was "dictatorial" and trying to turn doctors into "slaves to
the state". He groaned and shuddered.

From Estevan, Saskatchewan, Jamie left the highway and took
gravel back roads north for a while and stopped the car to get out and
stretch his legs. He walked along a border of summer fallow acreage
and shouldered into a persistent west wind that ruffled the green heads
of wheat in a nearby field. He smiled at the recollection of the familiar
cliché, that you can take the boy out of Saskatchewan but you can't take
the Saskatchewan out of the boy. Impertinent primroses and even a few
prairie tiger lilies winked at him from the roadside when he took a ham
sandwich out of his pocket and sat down to eat it while leaning on a

fence post. Gazing around at a cluster of grain elevators in the distance, prairie sentinels, it occurred to him that he probably could walk from here a hundred miles in a straight line in any direction and not bump into a tree not planted by man. He could hear his mother's voice saying, "I hate this emptiness, the desolation." But the wind continued to whistle its plaintive song to him and made him think of Roy, as often he did, of flying model airplanes into a breeze with his older brother and how he had loved to stamp his feet into the stubble, happy hearted, on a beautiful day like this.

It was the immensity of the cloudless pure blue sky that most got to him, stirred him. The drama of the landscape was always above. Jamie swiveled his head around the level circle of the horizon and considered the vast splendour of the sky that seemed as limitless as eternity. It made him feel very small and insignificant, but also singular and connected, and reminded him of the courage and hope and indomitable will of the people who first settled these farms, suffered through the bleak dust bowl years, and were now wresting better crops and a better future from this overpowering land under the biggest sky in the world. There was something clean and inspiriting about the soft sigh of wind and this infinite space. It was a land of stubborn optimism in which a man could dream big dreams.

The air had a scent of distance and rain and a coming storm. Above him a hawk soared and wheeled in the sky. Field mice had best beware.

XXII

When he reached Regina on June 5th he drove immediately to Milt's house on Argyle Crescent and, as instructed, prepared to let himself in with a key hidden in the garage, then grinned to find the house unlocked in the casual western way. Inside he saw the shelves of sports trophies, piles of LP records, the mantel-piece full of photographs of his mother and Roy and himself and a woman he didn't recognize, as well as the usual bachelor mess and clutter of pizza boxes, empty beer bottles, and pungent cigar butts in overflowing ashtrays. He liked the way Milt lived and smelled and filled his own space and didn't give a damn.

Milt turned up about six, chomping on a slim panatella cigar and carrying a case of twelve Molson's ale. They shook hands and laughed and then embraced and told each other how wonderful they looked, then Milt couldn't find an opener and snapped two bottle caps off with a pair of pliers and laughed again. Over a dinner of Chinese food at the W. K. they settled in and talked with ease as though they were two men who'd seen each other only the previous day.

"And how's my dad? Is he tolerably well?"

"Seems to be, yes, but still obsessed as ever with, you know, Commies. I saw him on 11th Avenue last week and he said he'd sold a couple of bulldozers and a gravel crusher to a big contractor, so he was upbeat. I'd say he'd had at least a head start on a snootful but he seemed more than cheery. Thinks he has the world by the tail on a downhill pull. Talked about working part-time for the KOD."

"What's that? Like the KKK?"

"Something like that, but terribly respectable among the right-wing guys. Stands for the Keep Our Doctors organization, a passel of Liberals and Chamber of Commerce types and reps of the doctors and a lot of other zealots who despise Woodrow Lloyd and want to protect us from the tyranny of medical insurance by presenting an allegedly non-party common front against the CCF. The KOD is new and very big, very loud. It's trying to whip up fears of pain and death with the threat of doctors leaving the province, although so far I've heard of only seven MDs who say they'll be getting out. But the strike is on, definitely, for July 1st, and the KOD is organizing rallies and slanging the evil socialists every day in the media. They have a lot of money and a lot of help and advice from eastern PR men and imported organizers and maybe, the word on the street has it, 'advisors' from the US, the AMA, the American Medical Association. There are a lot of rednecks among them, but also just plain worried citizens and terrified housewives, plus some sophisticated people from outside who know how to operate a pressure group."

"Wow. They sound pretty formidable, even scary."

"I'd say they are damn clever in their ability to manipulate public opinion. Certainly they've got people like your dad caught up in their campaign. Lorne seems to think it's time to go to the barricades, and if the KOD can get enough people behind them he's convinced that the government will cave in and withdraw the Act. He might be right, but I doubt it. So far Lloyd seems to be standing firm and the cabinet is behind him. They're sure taking a kicking, though."

"Damn it all, anyway. It's a shame."

"I'll tell you, Jamie, if you go out into the cafés and the streets tomorrow, and read the *Leader-Post* and listen to the radio, you'd think we were in a war zone or a revolution. I've never seen anything like it. The atmosphere is crackling with anger and fear and hate and I really think there could be violence at any time."

"Worse than the election campaign in 1960?"

"Much worse! It's a frenzy. It feels to me as though there's a boil or a carbuncle on the arse of the body politic that must somehow be lanced, and soon, if knocking heads is to be avoided. It's sad as hell to see people in the same family not speaking to each other over this."

"You're telling me?"

"Oh, right. Anyway, last week while you were travelling, the KOD organized a cavalcade of cars to converge on the legislative building to present a petition demanding 'that the medical care plan be delayed until it is acceptable to the medical profession.' They claimed the petition was signed by 45,000 citizens. The TV news gave it top coverage. The Premier came out on the front steps and tried to address the crowd but was interrupted and heckled and shouted down. The Liberal leader, Thatcher, appeared and was greeted by a rousing ovation and introduced as "the man who can tell us what to do now." He spoke in favour of either a plebiscite or a new election. A lot of radio and TV broadcasts led with his statement that, "This is a free democracy and we're not living in Russia yet.""

"Nice fellow," Jamie muttered.

"And when the government announced that they were preparing to fly in replacement doctors from Britain to provide services during the strike, the KOD denounced them as 'scabs' and MDs who couldn't make a living where they came from. At one of their rallies the KOD featured a large poster caricaturing a supposed replacement doctor with a large Semitic nose, a Chinese pigtail, and Arab clothing bearing a sign that read, 'Sask. Govt. Medicare Import'. No, they weren't afraid to play the race card. Jokes were circulated, like 'How can you tell an import doctor? By the medical badge he wears on his turban.' Or, 'How many replacement doctors does it take to treat a common cold? Three. One to read a medical text book, one to translate it into English, and one to offer a Kleenex and write the prescription.' Or, 'You can tell an import doctor by the diploma on his wall that reads, 'Graduate of the Negro Medical School of Lower Slobovia.' Nice, eh?"

"Charming," said Jamie. "Depressing. Let's go home to your place and watch the TV news."

"I like the way you call it 'home', me boy," Milt said with a smile. "But don't worry, it will all get worse."

For the next few days Jamie wandered around Regina with his eyes and ears open to reconnoitre and found that Milt had not exaggerated. There was no other topic of conversation but the coming strike and the situation seemed very tense. He phoned his father a couple of times and Lorne said he was "too busy" to see him. His attempts to interview doctors went nowhere, with the response invariably being that none would talk without the prior knowledge and consent of the College, and representatives of the College saying that they had no time available to assist academic research. He then tried to settle down to work on his thesis but had difficulty concentrating.

A quick trip to Prince Albert to visit the Slaters showed him that the apprehensions of the doctors' walkout were just as deep and distressing in the north as in the south. Dick was convinced that the government would falter and again delay implementation of the Act in the hope of re-opening negotiations or finding a mediator. This also seemed to be the opinion of several of his friends and former professors in Saskatoon. No one held out much hope of a rapid or easy settlement. The general view was that it all depended on which side blinked first, and not many were betting it would be the doctors.

Before he left Saskatoon, discouraged, Jamie spent two hours sitting and drowsing, not at his favourite place by the river, but at a different spot further north. The flow always seemed to draw him back and calm him. He'd read somewhere—was it in the great Wallace Stegner?—that a man is like a river, constantly moving and changing but steadily renewed. He relaxed enough to fall asleep on the grass.

Back in Regina he waited, as everyone waited, for the July 1 strike date.

On June 29 there was an announcement of the doctors' five-pronged policy, effective in two days:

1. All doctors' offices will be closed to patients.
2. No doctors will be available for home visits, except in the direst emergencies.
3. No telephone advice will be available from doctors.
4. There will be no prescription services.
5. Medical legal documents ... will not be procurable.
6. The patient will have no choice of doctor ... and it is likely that emergency services will be come more and more limited as the days progress.

When they read this statement on the TV screen, Milt turned to Jamie and said, "That's it. The game is up. Amazing that nothing whatsoever has been said about the Premier's offer, four days ago, that any doctor could practise outside the Act and could send his bill to the patient, who would then be reimbursed by the medical care plan. Both the patient and the doctor would be protected. Now what the flaming hell could be wrong about that?"

"Not a thing, so far as I can see. Unnecessarily awkward, but workable. You'd think that proposal, part of which they'd made earlier, of course, might have ended it all, broken the impasse, but I guess the truth is that the docs just aren't listening. They're so far out on a limb that they're saying NO to anything and everything. If the government suggested that the sun might rise in the east on July 1, the College would refuse to take their word for it and the KOD would swear it was a communist plot to crush our freedom. I dunno, Milt, I just don't know anymore. I guess we'll just have to wait for the first person to die for lack of medical treatment in early July. I'd bet dollars to donuts we won't have to wait long for that. I hope I'm wrong, but ...."

That first person proved to be Carl Derhousoff, a baby, nine months old. He was the youngest of a family of Hutterites from near Usherville.

Late on the night of June 30 the family realized the baby was seriously ill, and raced twenty-two miles on gravel roads to the town of Preeceville, but the doctor had left. In desperation the Derhousoffs drove on thirty-two miles to Canora, normally a busy four-doctor town, only to find that Canora had no emergency services and there was no doctor in the hospital. The family then drove another thirty-one miles to Yorkton, but the baby died before they arrived. With a large international press corps in Regina to report on the strike, this death grabbed headlines around the world. The *New York Times*, in a story widely copied in the US, reported that the doctor who confirmed the baby's death said the boy might have lived if he had received medical attention sooner.

This tragedy sparked an outburst of stories and editorials in the press that embarrassed the College and condemned the doctors. In the UK the London *Daily Mail* said that "when doctors strike and neglect patients, the voice of humanity protests." In the US the head of the legal medicine department at Harvard, while noting that he opposed "socialized medicine", nevertheless volunteered to investigate any death which "might be related to professional negligence by delinquent physicians …. It is my opinion that no doctor has the right to strike." The Toronto *Star*'s Val Sears and the *Globe and Mail*'s June Callwood filed reports critical of the doctors, and the *Financial Post*, hardly a leftist paper, published on its front page this stinging attack:

> The medical legislation … may or may not be good. But it is the law …. That's the way democracy works. But society finds revolutions, organized bands defying laws, intolerable …. [The strike] … is an outrageous assault on organized society …. The American Medical Association … may be delighted with the Saskatchewan performance. Is anybody else? The striking doctors in the months and years ahead will not be happy about their guinea-pigging for the AMA.

Jamie was pleased and relieved to review the reactions of the outside press at a hotel newsstand but knew they'd receive scant mention in the Sifton provincial media or be enough to end the strike. He phoned Dr. Abe Rivkin to learn his opinion and suggest lunch, and was surprised to be told that Helen was in town. "She phoned you in Toronto but missed you," said Abe, "and when she arrived in Regina she phoned your house. Your father was pretty cold to her and said he didn't know where you were. If you leave me a number I'm sure she'll call you back this evening. Got it. That's your Uncle Milt's house? I see. I'll tell her to ring you about six. All the best, Jamie. Hope to see you."

He arranged to pick her up at 6:30 and they greeted each other warmly. "How the hell are you, Jamie? I thought I'd lost track of you." "Good, good. I came out west four weeks ago to see the rumpus. You?" "Oh, I'm fat and sassy and working like stink. My editor in Vancouver remembered I was from Saskatchewan and sent me out to cover the strike. Big story. The major papers in Canada are all over it like mustard on a hot dog. And I'm hungry, let's go eat. I'm buying. I'll put you on my expense account as 'Interview with big deal Toronto professor who's an expert on health care.'" "I'm only a lecturer, Helen." "I know, I know, but my editor doesn't."

They had a grand reunion and a good dinner at the Bluebird Motor Inn with a bottle of Beaujolais and talked long into the evening about the medical imbroglio and how Tommy might have handled it differently, but decided that Lloyd was hanging tough in his dignified low-key manner and might yet weather the storm. Helen said there were 110 doctors from Britain and eastern Canada who'd already arrived to help out. Most of these staffed the community health clinics that were springing up in the major cities. "They might make the local docs think twice about losing patients and losing income," Jamie said. On impulse they phoned Dick in Prince Albert and urged him to come down to meet them. He said he was too pre-occupied with aldermanic work and helping Dr. Orville Hjertas to organize a community clinic sponsored by a labour union and some local co-ops, but he'd keep in touch and be glad to meet them later in Saskatoon. There'd be a big KOD rally in Saskatoon on July 6th, he said, and his curiosity was pushing him to attend. "Might could," said Jamie, "and Helen would get a story out of it."

She did. They sat at the press table in the gym of St. Paul's High School and listened as the mass rally of 500 supporters was addressed by a lawyer and three doctors. One of the MDs observed that the previously difficult situation was worsening because in the critical emergency services not as many doctors volunteered as had been hoped for.

Much the strongest of many denunciations of the CCF government was made by Father Athol Murray of Wilcox, a feisty seventy-year-old priest. His speech was carried live over a network of private radio stations. "A wave of hatred is sweeping Saskatchewan," he shouted. "There has been death, there will be violence. This thing may break out into violence and bloodshed any day now, and God help us it doesn't." He paused dramatically for effect, tearing off his coat and clerical collar.

Jamie closed his eyes and held his head in shock. Dick leaned over and whispered to Helen, "Now there's a gentle, loving Christian message from a man of the cloth, eh?" Helen only blinked and continued scribbling.

"There are Reds here!" the priest cried. "I can't see them, I can smell them. You Communists may think we're naïve and hollow-chested but we gave a hundred thousand boys fighting for the freedom you're fighting against. You Reds, I want you to know that we're as proud as hell to be Canadians. ... Tell those bloody Commies to go to hell .... I loathe the welfare state and I love the free-swinging freedom. I am seventy and I'll never ask you for the Old Age Pension—to hell with it—I want to be free!"

Helen whispered to Jamie, "Maybe he hasn't heard of how the Catholic Church coddles its retired priests, do you think?" "I hope they let this one starve," Jamie replied.

"We are living in tragic times .... Doctors are leaving Swift Current and we're proud of them. These doctors are great guys." Toward the end of his speech, he stated: "I wouldn't be surprised if someone put a bullet in me—I'm as likely to get it as Woodrow Lloyd."

"Damn," said Dick, "I forgot to bring my gun." "Don't even say that word," Jamie moaned. "That's all we need, and a demented priest who thinks he's Billy the Kid."

When the rally was over, Helen got a quote from the president of the KOD citing the priest's "long record of service to people of all denominations in the province", and then rushed off to find a telephone to file copy. The boys waited outside for her, smoking cigarettes. Dick said, "Father Athol is aptly named, wouldn't you thay?" When Helen came back they went downtown to a speakeasy she knew on 3rd Street and rounded off their night.

Dick returned to Prince Albert and Helen and Jamie drove back to Regina, speculating on whether the next big KOD rally there could out-do the one they'd just witnessed. It was to be on July 11 on the grounds of the legislative building and promised to be a real rip snorter. Advertising for the event began to appear in newspapers across the province on July 6. Dentists and most pharmacies announced they would close so their staff and patients could join the march on the capital. The Retail Merchants Association said their employees were free to attend the mass rally. On the two days prior to the march, TV, radio, and newspapers were flooded with KOD releases and requests for donations of 'Dollars for Freedom'. The KOD's 'Protest and Petition' to be presented to the government filled full page ads in the larger newspapers:

> ... *Assembled on these grounds on which stand the Legislative Buildings of Saskatchewan, consecrated to the 'ideal of self-government ... in a free society;*
>
> *Dedicated to the concept that no ruler in a free society may in conscience coerce a minority group of citizens ... [or] discriminate against*

them in their profession ....

... compulsion and coercion are subversive .... The government
alone is responsible .... [It should] suspend the operation of the Act ....

... Citizens protest the callous disregard ... shown to the expressed
will of the citizens .... We protest the dictatorial and arbitrary provisions
of the ... Act ....

July 11 was a typically hot sunny summer's day in Saskatchewan.
Helen and Jamie were apprehensive and found an open window in the
legislative building where they could watch the scene below. "There's
a big police presence to keep order," Helen noted. "Two officers told
me that there was a fear of violence. They say the KOD expects 30,000
or 40,000 marchers on the grounds, maybe more." "If that many turn
out," said Jamie, "the campaign will be said to be a success, and the
government might be intimidated, lose heart. Dear god, I hope not. Is
it too late to pray for rain?"

"Look, over there," Helen pointed. Two young men on the edge of
the crowd carried pro-medicare placards. "Those boys are going to be
roughed up." Police intervened to protect them and another group of
government supporters, amid shouts of 'Commies', and 'Go back to the
Kremlin'. Two girls carried effigies of Tommy and of Premier Lloyd,
hanged by the neck, with a banner between them reading, 'Down with
dictators'. There were incidents of pushing and shoving all over the
grounds, any one of which might have triggered fist fights or worse. In a
nearby window Jamie heard a reporter from the *Globe and Mail* speaking
rapidly into a tape recorder:

Hundred of cars converged on the provincial capital ... to present a
petition .... Sincere attempts were made [by the KOD] to keep order
.... But at one point the ugly temper showed through .... Two students
... walked with pro-medicare signs .... Angry demonstrators moved in
on them .... A knot of demonstrators hemmed in [the two boys] and told

them to drop dead, or go back to Russia .... The group taunting the two
also railed at reporters who interviewed the youths ....

A watching US television network correspondent said: 'This is
just like covering the anti-integration movement in the Southern United
States. They're the same kind of people! ...'

"There's Ross Thatcher and most of his Liberal caucus," Helen pointed. "I think he's trying to get them to open the main front doors. Let's run down and see." They found Mr. Thatcher, who had discovered that as usual the entrance to the legislative chamber was locked when the House was not sitting, kicking at the doors vigorously for the benefit of the TV cameras. "We think these are tactics one would expect to find in Russia or Cuba," Thatcher proclaimed loudly to reporters. "Its just another indication that freedom is being extinguished in Saskatchewan." Jamie thought the Liberal leader was engaging in theatrics and making a farce of the legislature.

The KOD succeeded in presenting their petition and getting lead time on the TV news. But the march and 'mass rally' was a failure. The estimate of most reporters and the Canadian Press wire service was that only 4,000 people showed up. Jamie and Helen whooped and hugged each other when they heard the numbers. "I think we've got 'em," Helen laughed. "I think we're home free."

"Lookin' good," Jamie agreed with a broad grin. "Maybe not the clincher, but we're lookin' good for now."

The doctors and the KOD, clearly surprised and disappointed, never regained their momentum.

Senior spokesmen for the Canadian Medical Association were increasingly disenchanted with the reactions in the press and in some of the strike leaders as the profession began to have difficulty maintaining the strike. Some doctors began quietly to re-open their practices. The vigour and confidence of the KOD began to diminish and the atmosphere lightened noticeably. Lorne McRae sulked and cursed and went on another bender.

The government began to fly in not only more replacement doctors but also a mediator that the College tentatively agreed to, a prominent British physician from the upper house of Parliament, Lord Taylor. A tall, imposing, spirited and shaggy-browed figure and a veteran of many medical disputes in the UK, Taylor set up shop in the Bessborough Hotel in Saskatoon on July 18, moving briskly between representatives of the two conflicting sides, salving egos and spreading optimism.

Helen phoned Jamie on the 19th, chirping that she had found the AMA 'advisors', like the US military 'advisors' then in Vietnam. How had she located them? Wasn't really much of a problem after she'd thought about it, she said, merely a matter of sweet-talking a night clerk on the desk of the Hotel Saskatchewan and thumbing through the register until she found, together, two names with home addresses in Chicago, a Dr. Abrahamson and a Mr. Connelley, probably a public relations man. "I've requested an interview with Abrahamson and I'm having drinks with him in the hotel bar in half an hour. Why don't you fall by, just casually, you know, and I'll introduce you as a professor so he'll think you're harmless." "Whatever you say, Helen, but I doubt he'll talk."

He did, but very carefully.

"I take it you're a journalist, Miss Rivkin."

"Yes, doctor, from Vancouver, but originally from the Bronx, an American like yourself and also Jewish, a friendly scribbler. Fascinated by the important conflict here, but pretty much finished my assignment and getting ready to go back to BC. Can we talk a bit about the strike? That's why you're here, I suppose."

"Oh, no, I was just passing through and stopped off to meet some medical colleagues, that's all. Interesting situation, though, I'm sure you'd agree. I've had some friendly chats, nothing more. What are you drinking?"

"Um, vodka martini, please, straight up, with a twist."

"And may I assume that one of your twists is to carry a micro tape recorder in your handbag? Rather obvious, you know, when you were fumbling for a pad and pencil. So, I'll mention that I'll sue you, of course, and your newspaper, discredit you both and deny we've ever met, if you even think of quoting me directly on anything concerning these local events. No point in trying to stir up difficulties, now is there?"

"Just a general 'backgrounder', then, entirely off the record."

"That seems agreeable, yes."

"Well, your organization, the AMA, has had another success recently in squelching President Kennedy's health insurance bill. You're happy about that, no doubt?"

"Content, quite content. The President and his rather obstreperous brothers got a bit carried away, I think, and over-stepped what I'd call the bounds of political prudence. We felt we ought to point out some short-comings in his plan, that's all."

Jamie appeared at their table. Helen introduced him as professor McRae from Toronto.

"And is your university a hot bed of radicalism too, professor?"

"Not really, no. I'm here for part of the summer because I was born and raised here. Great place, this, great people."

"And some of these people tend to get over-excited when they are whipped up by pinko propaganda, wouldn't you say?"

"That's one way of putting it. I'd put it differently."

Uneasy, Helen asked, "Did your friend Connelley help with the KOD campaign? I'd guess he might be the one who drafted a lot of the news releases, and probably the Petition and Protest statement for instance. Would that be right?"

"My colleague has a lot of talent for cutting to the heart of an issue, and organizing for a common front that's not merely the vehicle of a single political interest or viewpoint, and sharing the benefits of our experience. As for the Petition, I'd say it was the result of several hands and minds working together in the common cause of freedom."

"Ah, yes," said Helen, "but do you think that people are really free if they lack access to medical care?"

"Surely all they need is to buy normal private health insurance from respectable companies in the business. That's the American way, the free enterprise way, the great pillar of our free society."

"Seems to me unfortunate," said Jamie, "that something like a million Americans declare bankruptcy every year because they can't pay their health care bills or afford expensive private insurance that offers only limited coverage anyway."

"I don't have statistics on that. Seems to me your figure is over-blown. But if people refuse to work hard and purchase for themselves what they need, they might naturally get into trouble."

"I see," said Helen. "And so I suppose you've learned a lot from your experience here that can be applied to the US when you get back to Chicago?"

"From my observations, yes. There were some things here that I wish had been done somewhat differently. However, this little bonfire will burn itself out soon enough. People will come to their senses. And when the lamentable John Kennedy and his like mount similar efforts toward socialist regimentation in the US in the future, as they will, we'll simply use the same approach we've always used. We'll muster the support of big business and the larger insurance companies and the reliable Republican party, all right-thinking people, and be prepared to spend a little money on advertising and advocacy in support of our cause."

"Propaganda?" put in Jamie.

"Information. Clear-headed presentation of facts and arguments. It's not at all difficult, you know. Just remember that big business is the foundation of American society, and that newspapers and the electronic media, particularly with the growing concentration of ownership, are very big businesses indeed. We tend to agree with each other on basic values and see things eye to eye. I'd have to concede that here in your province the press may have over-played their case a little, got a bit heavy-handed, but that may have been a necessary reaction to the false ideology and so-called 'neutrality' of your CBC, which was inconveniently intrusive. But in the US, where public broadcasting has been, ah, marginalized, the people don't have that sort of distraction, which makes our campaigning and educational efforts much easier."

Jamie smiled ruefully. "It was your Mark Twain, a sensible fellow, who wrote that there are all sorts of laws to protect freedom of the press, but none to protect us from the press."

"Well, Twain was an eccentric and disputatious fellow, surely, just a humourist. But for now let's merely agree to disagree, change the topic, and have another drink, shall we? Here's to Canadian-American friendship. Long may we co-operate and collaborate for a better world. Freedom, that's the thing!"

Dammit all, Helen thought, here I get an exclusive interview and a scoop, even get it on tape, and I can't use it unless my paper is willing to get its ass sued off. Fat chance. She gulped the rest of her martini. Only half listening, she heard Dr. Abrahamson ask Jamie what he taught in Toronto? Economics? Well, well. And why did he take such an interest in medicare?

"Partly the economics of it," Jamie replied, "but mostly I'd say it was because of Tommy Douglas. And the Sermon on the Mount. Brotherhood."

"Ah. An idealist. Well, you're young. You'll learn. Do have another drink. As we Americans like to say, I'm buying."

XXIII

As the doctors' strike began to erode and support for the KOD went into decline Jamie had a strong sense that the most menacing part of the storm was dissolving. Lord Taylor had an easier time with his negotiations. He realized that both parties wanted to end the dispute peacefully and the doctors mainly wanted to save face, making it less difficult to smooth the path toward a settlement. His prestige and his ebullient personality helped to pave the way. Alternatively pleading and demanding, cursing and cajoling, sometimes speaking softly and sometimes thumping the table, he worked with lawyers for both sides for many days and finally pressed them into reaching an accord. The Saskatoon Agreement was signed in the Bessborough Hotel on the banks of the South Saskatchewan River on July 23, ending the strike. Happily it ended not with a bang but with huge sighs of relief all around. The legislature was convened for a special session in early August and the (mostly minor) amendments were passed into law. Medicare had come to Saskatchewan.

Dick grinned and poured a large rye and water as he watched the TV broadcast at 12:45 p.m. that confirmed the Agreement. Milt and Jamie each hoisted a glass of wine in a toast to the settlement and pounded each other on the back as they watched the same broadcast on CBC. The next day Helen, tired but elated after writing a long wrap-up, phoned both Dick and Jamie, saying she was flying back to Vancouver that afternoon.

Before he left Regina, Jamie had a much postponed but most cheerful lunch with Dr. Rivkin. They sat in a corner of the modest cafeteria of the Department of Health where the mood was a lot more upbeat than it had been three weeks earlier.

"This is what I hoped could be achieved, what I hoped to be part of," said Abe, "when I came to Saskatchewan all those years ago. For a while there, in late June, I wasn't at all sure that we'd make it, but now I feel it was all worth while, that I had a small part in a truly pioneering venture and was privileged to be here. It makes me feel damn good, really satisfied, let me tell you."

"Will you and Rose go back to the 'States now?"

"I'm not sure. We like it here. We've sort of put down roots, you know? It's a good place to live. I'm glad Helen was raised here. I've thought about it, a lot, but I'm not sure I could just pick up and go back to New York where I'd find the atmosphere less, um, congenial. And as long as I can squeeze in—he laughed—a few weeks every winter in Florida …."

"I know what you mean. It does get chilly."

"What about you? Going back to Toronto in a few days, you say?"

"Yup. It takes me three days or less on the road, so I'll have all of August to catch up on work. It's that damned thesis. But now that I don't have to spend half as much sweat on lecture preparation and I've got this strike off my mind, I'll find the time."

"Sure, just bash it out and get it in. Not all that important, I believe, not to fret about. It's the publications that you can distill out of it later that will count. You might even consider writing about the strike and the Saskatchewan experience after you have the degree in hand."

"That's occurred to me. Once things are settled down and I've got more perspective on the events, I think I'll try."

"Good. With the thesis done and a publication or two, you'll be set up as one of the few, the very few, health economists in the country, able to write your own ticket."

"I'll always be grateful to you, Abe, for helping me get started on all this."

"And we'll both always be grateful to Tommy. Without him ...." Abe paused to reflect. "But how do you think it will all play out in a few years? I'd be interested in your predictions."

"Oh, I'm not sure. As Yogi Berra said, 'Prediction is always hard, especially about the future.' I do expect medicare will be very popular, probably spread throughout the country within the decade. Even more popular than the hospital or auto insurance plans. Odd how a so-called socialist party is such a champion of that most conservative method, insurance, don't you think? Anyway, the gossip I hear from Ottawa is that the Royal Commission on health care, appointed last year by Diefenbaker and the Conservatives—and you know that the chairman, Mr. Justice Emmett Hall of the Supreme Court, is a bright and honest man—will recommend that Canada follow the Saskatchewan model. That will outrage the Americans, but should be a great help here."

"And the doctors. Do you think they'll be reconciled?"

"Quickly, I think, yes. They'll find it efficient and convenient to receive their fee-for-service from a single payer. Without worrying about collecting their fees and bad debts any more, looks to me as though medical incomes will rise, in fact, likely by at least a third."

"Some of the doctors are still pretty bitter."

"Yeh, it was like a wind-driven prairie fire that flashes through the stubble, burning away suddenly, and leaving lots of seared and scorched earth behind. My thoughts on that would be to have the Premier and the Minister of Health make a few speeches saying that the quarrel was never with the rank and file MDs, not with the ordinary dedicated physicians, but with only a few over-anxious ideologues in the leadership cadré, medical politicians who whipped up fears and hugely exaggerated the conflict, making it adversarial instead of the co-operative effort it should have been. Wouldn't hurt to make nice and downplay the slanging and stroke the docs a bit. They're mostly very good people."

"Might help, yes. So in general, Jamie, you see the future as rosy?"

"You know better than that, Abe. Of course not. There'll be

problems, when are there not? Cost will climb, escalate rapidly. We won on insurance, but don't forget that we insured and helped to perpetuate a highly inefficient health care delivery system. Surely solo practice is obsolete. We'll need more preventive care. We'll need more multi-discipline walk-in clinics, more physicians' assistants, less conflict between the MDs and the other health care professions. Probably you've read Dr. Rutstein, a Harvard professor of medicine, who writes about the 'tangled and torn web of medical services', the 'conflicting and duplicating activities' of the unplanned system, the inadequate research on how to deliver integrated services better and more cheaply. There's the next set of problems, wouldn't you say?"

"I would, yes. And I don't know Rutstein; I'll look him up. But it amuses me that the tables have turned since your undergrad days, and now you're instructing me what to read. Mazel tov, dear boy. But now I must be getting back to work. There was something else, though. Yes. Almost forgot. Here's a clipping Helen sent me yesterday, asked me to give you a copy. It was written by her popular columnist friend on the Vancouver *Sun*, Jack Scott, during the 1960 election campaign on medicare.

> *This man Douglas is—well, how shall I put it? He's a good deed in a naughty world. He's a breath of clean prairie air in a stifling climate of payola and chicanery and double-talk and pretence, global and local.*
>
> *Forget the politics. He's a man who wanted to do something for the improvement of the human race. He chose the method that seemed best to him, quarrel with it if you will. He was motivated by an ideal.*
>
> *To call him a politician, as you'd call Wacky Bennett or Diefenbaker politicians, is to insult him. He was and is a dreamer and a humanitarian, incorruptible, genuine and intellectually honest.*

"Thanks, Abe, I'll hold on to that. And thanks for lunch. My very best to Helen."

XXIV

Jamie's next trip to Regina was unexpected.

He had hunkered down to work as soon as he returned to Toronto and, during August, written over eighty pages, the last three chapters of his delinquent thesis. In September he had it typed and submitted, chatted his way through a perfunctory oral exam, and was told that the degree would be conferred at the fall convocation.

Greatly relieved, he had written about the completion of his efforts to his father but, as anticipated, he received no reply. Meanwhile, he'd phoned Milt to say all was well and written postcards to Helen and Dick and Norm Ward telling them that he'd finally got the thesis off his back and was enjoying teaching more. Milt in particular was delighted and sent along a welcome cheque with his congratulations. Jamie spent part of the money on a spiffy new leather briefcase and paying off his bill at the bookstore. He took a new girlfriend named Maureen out to dinner at La Chaumière and thought the university was a wonderful place after all.

The next communication he received from Milt was an October phone call to his office just before a three o'clock class. "I have news," his uncle said cryptically.

"I hope it's that you're coming down to Toronto for a visit?"

"No. Nothing like that. You're coming here. I'm sorry to tell you that Lorne died suddenly last night." Long pause. "Jamie, are you there? Something about a blocked aorta and heart failure. You'll want to catch an evening flight, tonight. I'll meet you at the airport."

Taken aback, Jamie stumbled through his three o'clock, found a helpful colleague to cover his Friday morning class, phoned to book a ticket, then called Milt back to say which flight he'd be on.

Good as his word, Milt met the plane and, as they drove to his house, recounted all he knew about the time and cause of death and that Lorne hadn't been well for several weeks. Jamie merely nodded a lot and said little. At Milt's place his uncle poured a stiff scotch for each of them and said they'd order in pizza later. They talked long into the night but in an evasive and desultory way, recounting many old memories, many of which seemed to revolve more around Jean and Roy than about Lorne. Neither of them was looking forward to the next couple of days. All Jamie could think to say, over and over, was, "Such a disappointed man. Such a disappointed life. He never seemed to have much fun, you know?" Soon he mumbled that he didn't feel much like eating, and went off to bed.

The next day Milt stayed with him and guided him through the necessaries of hiring a minister, arranging for flowers and, in the absence of a will, deciding on cremation. He'd rather scatter the ashes—where? This man never seemed to have any permanent location or center to his unhappy life. That question and several others could be faced after the ceremony.

The funeral service went well enough and the reception at the house swam by in a haze of well-intentioned smiles and good wishes, mostly from people he'd swear he'd never seen before in his life. Was this what his mother's funeral had been like? He believed so, but hoped not.

Uncle Milt remained by his side throughout the day, then slipped away from the end of the reception with the promise to return and pick him up for dinner about seven, leaving Jamie time to browse through the house and collect his thoughts while two kindly neighbour ladies cleaned up and stacked glasses. He sat on the back steps for a while in the brisk autumn air and smoked several cigarettes.

By seven-thirty they were seated at a quiet table on the side at the W. K. Chinese restaurant, sipping beer and ordering Jamie's favourite dishes, won ton soup, shrimp in lobster sauce, Cantonese chow mein, sweet and sour pork, mushroom steamed rice, even though he had little appetite. During dinner both seemed pre-occupied and said very little, but when they returned to Milt's house they lit a fire in the fireplace, kicked off their shoes, put their feet up, and sampled a bottle of Cragganmore single malt.

"Could you believe the guff spouted by that porridge-faced minister? All that blithering about Heaven as though it were a desirable place. Can you imagine anything more boring than floating around on a cloud playing a harp? It'd be like listening to Lawrence Welk through all eternity. Dear god. And that blather about him being popular, a man's man, eh? He even said something about dad being proud of me. As if."

"I think he was, Jamie. He just didn't have any gift for expressing his emotions. In his own way he had feelings too. Crabbed, I'd say, beaten down and hugely disillusioned by the way life had treated him. Don't be too hard on him. I know he disagreed with you on most things, and buffeted you more than he should have, gave you a hard time I'd say, but you've got to see things more from his perspective. Smacked by the depression, not enough money, moving from job to job and embarrassed by a bankruptcy, maybe wrong but stung by his politics, wounded by the loss of Roy, and then Jean's death. How much shit can be piled on a man? I mean, think about it. Life dealt him some pretty bad hands, and he had trouble playing them."

"You're right, Milt. What you say is right. It's just so hard for me to understand or accept. All I knew as a boy was that the results weren't always pleasant. His disapproval was always a burden. It hurt. I mean, his coldness to me, his treatment of my mother …. But it's true, he never seemed to catch a break or find any good luck, poor bugger."

"He had his own private demons, his own problems. Doesn't everybody? Jean was my cousin and I loved her, but she wasn't exactly an easy woman to live with, not accepting, not earthy or sensuous, not my idea of an ideal wife."

"How do you mean, 'not sensuous'? What are you saying? I always knew that their marriage was a disaster, but surely ...."

"You must understand that Jean's upbringing was terribly old-fashioned, Victorian. Her mother was a prude and a bitch. Jean's notion of marital relations, er, sex, was that it was a duty toward procreation, full stop. And even Lorne knew that with the depression dragging on he couldn't afford more children, more mouths to feed. Look, I'll be blunt. I doubt that Lorne ever got laid—at home, at least—after Roy was born."

That took a moment to register with Jamie. Harsh stuff. "But, but, I was born, wasn't I? Five years after Roy, so you *can't* be right about this. You shock me Milt! I, I'm ...."

"There's more, lad, much more. It's well past time that I told you the full story about all this. Give me a minute to compose myself. It's hard for me to find the words. Pour me another scotch and let me think how to say what I need to say."

"To say what? For godssake, what? Maybe you've said enough."

"No. With Lorne gone now I can open the lid and get it all out. While he was alive I was sworn to silence, bloody awful as it often was to look the other way and keep quiet. Please, don't make it harder for me by getting angry."

"You know I could never be angry with you, Milt, but I'm startled as hell at what you said. I can't understand why you are saying it. What secret? Why a silence? You're not making sense to me. Sorry, but you're not."

"All right, I guess not, but I'm trying. Believe me, I'm trying." He stopped. Looked away. Rubbed his forehead and cleared his throat. "Jamie, my promise no longer holds, with Lorne gone. Jean gone too, so I can say it. Listen to me. Jean was not your mother. You were adopted. Loved, but not Jean's child. Adopted. Lorne, may he rest in peace, was not your father. We both have to level with each other and think about this differently. Lorne was not your real father."

"What? I can't believe this! What are you saying? It doesn't, I mean, it can't be …."

"Dammit all, I've rehearsed this speech for years and now I can't get the words to come out right. Roy was your cousin."

"My cousin? Why, I mean, how …?"

"You're not making this any easier for me. Roy was the son of Lorne and Jean. You are my son. I'm your father."

"My father? *You* are my *father*?"

Jamie stared at him in open-mouthed astonishment. Couldn't utter a word for minutes. He felt quietly exultant. It was as though something warm had exploded in his chest. His heart pounded and his blood raced as the questions fell all over each other in his head. Then he smiled broadly. They broke the crackling tension by both getting up and laughing and hugging.

"You're not distressed? I hope that's good news to you. It always has been for me, but it was a torment not to be able to say anything."

"Distressed? Wow, I couldn't be happier! Or more stunned. It's like a dream to me, a dream come true. Really! But you've got some tall explaining to do, Milt. Dad." He grinned again. "Why the secrecy? I mean, I mean, this is all so stupefying to me, I can't … ?"

"Well, I've told you before that I was once married, to Laura, a wonderful woman. She died in childbirth, but the baby survived. I named him James Thomas Milton. You. But I was distraught and I guess not very competent with the infant. Didn't know how. He – you – cried a lot and was losing weight. The doctor said there was nothing wrong. I tried to hire a nanny, but that didn't seem to work out.

"Jean moved in for a few days to help me out, but couldn't neglect her own family, and so after much discussion and a lot of hand-wringing we mutually decided that the baby should go home with her for a while at least. I had no intention of re-marrying and I guess I stayed morose and depressed over my wife's death for a time. Soon Jean began to talk of adopting you so that you'd have a proper home and family and an older brother and not be subjected to the fumbling care of a bachelor who couldn't always be at home.

"Lorne wasn't entirely keen on the idea of adoption. At Jean's insistence, we negotiated an arrangement which seemed, well, satisfactory at the time, although later I had second thoughts …. I wanted you close by so that I could see you and take an interest and watch you grow up, so adoption with Jean as the mother seemed the right thing, and you understand that I wanted only what was best for you.

"Lorne, as I say, had doubts and worries, fair enough that he should. He thought we should draw up a formal contract in addition to the adoption papers, and I agreed. I had to promise him that I would not interfere with his family, remain just an uncle, pay Jean a small amount monthly for your keep, and also swear that I would stay totally silent about our arrangement, which later proved hard, and that I would not play the rich uncle and spoil or over-indulge you, or Roy. I'm sure that the whole deal and his own strained finances embarrassed him, and doubtless he didn't entirely trust me to keep up my end of the bargain. So I made promises and swore and signed the deal as though it was Magna Carta—which to me, of course, it bloody well was.

"Is that all clear enough? Does that make sense to you?"

"Clear and perfect sense to me, Dad."

"I'm grateful and relieved to hear you call me 'Dad'."

"I'll continue to use 'Milt' if you prefer."

"No, please, 'Dad'. It's been a long time coming. I think Jean would be pleased, too."

After a long and companionable silence in which they both stared into the fireplace, Jamie said that he'd have a lot of questions later, when he'd thought about it all, but maybe not yet. It was too soon, too startling, for him to comprehend how drastically the center of his life had shifted. Are there really any certainties in this world where the things you are confidant you know turn out to be illusions? He felt as though he'd thrown open a previously concealed window and seen a fresh breeze lift the curtains.

"I'm enormously relieved to have that off my mind," Milt sighed. "As you can imagine there were plenty of times when I'd have liked to do more, certainly spend more on you and on Roy, but in general—well, there was that one small lapse about spending on travel to England—I was able to keep my word to Lorne till now. I will mention that there's a trust fund in your name, available any time, particularly now that you're Dr. McRae. Unless you'd like me to change your name on the account to 'James Milton'?"

"It would mean changing my name on the driver's licence and the passport and some other documents. Let's take some time later to think about that. Just to shift my understanding and my perspective will take me a while." It's one damn strange night, he mused, when you're not even sure of your own name anymore, when you're told you're not who you think you are. But he was exhilarated. The more he tried to sort out his flux of emotions, the more he felt like a cork long caught in rocks under water and suddenly released, that bobbed surging to the surface.

"And don't you want to ask about the money? Some filthy lucre can come in handy to a young man. Maybe you'll have children of your own one day."

"I hope and intend that, but I also hope the numbers of dollars are not too, um, troublesome to cope with, not too distracting."

"Hardly. With the rate of inflation these days you might not consider it a large sum. I did get lucky with some stocks after the War, though, things like Coca Cola and IBM and a few others, so even as an underpaid professor they won't be holding any tag days for you. There's plenty for a new car, for example, from interest without touching capital. I think knowing that there's a bit of money available can give a man more assurance, more confidence, and I never thought you had enough of that."

"Holy cow," Jamie exclaimed. "Thank you, thanks a million."

"Oh, let's not talk in millions, me boy, but maybe enough to give you some cushion, and pleasure to us both. And one other thing. You might be amused. You are part owner of a motel. Yup. I thought it only fair and appropriate, back in '46, that I should buy a couple of shares for each of you and Roy in the Bluebird Motor Inn and Lounge." Jamie got a chuckle out of *that*. "As you'd expect, it still does good business. I'll be transferring Roy's shares to you shortly, now that we have this financial nonsense out on the table."

They sat without speaking for a while longer. Jamie had a heartening sense that his life's range of possibilities had been kicked up a couple of notches. Finally Milt got up and poked the fireplace and suggested they go to bed. "It's been a long evening," he said, "and you've had more than enough revelations for one day."

"Yes. I'll say! My head is still spinning."

"Should I take you down to the bank with me Monday morning and attend to some of those things?"

"Thanks, but no. Tomorrow's Sunday and I really should get back. Classes in the morning Monday as usual. I'm vastly obliged to you, tremendously grateful, but you've given me a whole lot more to think about than the bank. We can attend to that at Christmas. I'll fly here for the holidays if that's all right."

"Of course, most certainly. Delighted. Bring a friend, or a girlfriend if you like. And what will you do back in Toronto, apart from teach? Do you have plans?"

"Absolutely. I've decided to start work on a book on Tommy and medicare and the doctors' strike. Too important not to write about, and better while it's all fresh in my mind. It's a story that really matters. That's what I'll do. Yes."

And he did.